## "What's happening?"

Guy's grip on Maude's arm stopped her and brought her back under the rain-battered awning.

"I've got a patient coming in."

He pulled her closer and held her by both arms. Reflexively she raised her hands, then balled them into fists instead of putting them on his chest as she wanted to do. She tried to concentrate on a raindrop trickling down her face, but all she could see was the darkness of his eyes and all she could hear was the pounding of her heart. She needed to kiss this man.

Slowly, as if time had no meaning, he lowered his mouth to hers and the fire burst inside her. Flames raged through her senses and threatened to consume everything except her desire for him—until the doctor took over.

She pushed back. "I've got to go."

Dear Reader,

Rugged western Montana urged me to tell a story amid its soaring mountains and sweeping pine forests. To do so, I needed characters who would stand out against a backdrop of magnificent scenery. Maude and Guy, two doctors so wounded they could not heal themselves, fit the roles well.

Enemies in the past and now touched by the same tragedy, they must forgive each other—then forgive themselves. When they do, the passion between them becomes love. With love as big as all Montana, they make a family for a little girl orphaned by the same tragic loss.

Sometimes life hurts. I believe it is the pain that shows us how brightly the joy can shine.

I loved taking these three "injured by life" people and, in my first book for Harlequin, molding a fiercely loving family who couldn't imagine living without one another. I hope you love them, too.

I'd love to hear from you. Visit my Web site at www.marybrady.net or write to me at MaryBrady@marybrady.net.

Regards and happy reading,

*Mary Brady*

# HE CALLS HER DOC
*Mary Brady*

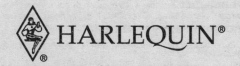

HARLEQUIN®

TORONTO • NEW YORK • LONDON
AMSTERDAM • PARIS • SYDNEY • HAMBURG
STOCKHOLM • ATHENS • TOKYO • MILAN • MADRID
PRAGUE • WARSAW • BUDAPEST • AUCKLAND

Recycling programs
for this product may
not exist in your area.

ISBN-13: 978-0-373-71561-9
ISBN-10:    0-373-71561-7

HE CALLS HER DOC

Copyright © 2009 by Mary L. Biebel.

www.eHarlequin.com

**Printed in U.S.A.**

## ABOUT THE AUTHOR

Mary Brady lives in the Midwest and considers road trips into the rest of the continent to be a necessary part of life. When she's not out exploring, she helps run a manufacturing company and has a great time living with her handsome husband, her super son and one cheeky little bird.

For my husband and son, with whom I make my own fiercely loving—and laughing—family of three.

## Acknowledgments

My thanks to the people of Montana, who have never been anything but welcoming to me and who won't know where to find the town of St. Adelbert, because it exists only in my mind.

And to Dr. Gillian Rickmeier, who selflessly answered my questions about the medical field. That said, any errors in this book—especially errors concerning medical issues—are mine and mine alone.

# CHAPTER ONE

MAUDE DEVANE, M.D., bypassed her crisp white lab coat and slipped on the one with a couple of badges of courage stained faintly into the fabric. Collar turned to the chill of the sunny June morning, she stepped out onto the ramp of the Wm. Avery Clinic's emergency entrance. Somewhere under the biggest, bluest of Montana skies a man had fallen from a horse.

And she was ready, make that eager, to help her first patient in her brand-new solo practice.

On cue, the Squat-D Ranch's red pickup truck careened around a corner and raced up Main Street. Traffic in the tiny mountain town of St. Adelbert made way as if they knew the passenger was unconscious.

Some of them probably did.

The truck lurched up the ramp and fishtailed to a halt, engulfing Maude in the smell of oily exhaust.

Curly Martin's great-grandson Jimmy burst out the driver's side door. "He still ain't talking to me, Dr. DeVane!"

The bear-size seventeen-year-old barreled around toward the passenger side. As Maude reached the dusty truck, she leaned in to see the ninety-two-year-old rancher slumped against the door.

"Jimmy, get back in the truck." Maude conveyed calm in her command. "And hold him in position. Don't move him at all, especially his head." And if they were all very lucky, the old man was not already paralyzed.

Jimmy dashed back around and scrambled into the cab. As he cradled his great-grandfather in his giant hands, Maude opened the door and reached in to feel for a pulse.

"Is he dead?" Jimmy peered at her from under the bill of his faded green cap.

She gave him a quick smile. "He's alive, Jimmy." Curly Martin, icon, epitome of cowboy in these parts, was not going down to a spill from a horse, not if she had any say.

She patted Curly's chest. "Mr. Martin." No response. "Curly, open your eyes." She rubbed her knuckles into the man's breastbone hard enough to awaken a sleeping person. The man remained still, his lips a pale slash in his tanned face.

"Keep holding him just like that, Jimmy. I need to put a protective collar on his neck."

"I'm here, Dr. DeVane," a woman's quiet voice said from behind her.

Maude turned to the dark-haired, scrubs-clad, on-call nurse holding the stiff cervical collar in her hand. Maude smiled. "Thanks for getting here so quickly, Abby."

"Carolyn will be here soon," Abby said of the tech on call.

Maude nodded and then bent down to speak into Curly's "good" ear. "Mr. Martin, I'm going to put a safety collar around your neck," she said in the event he could actually hear her. After stabilizing his neck, the three of them lifted the unconscious man onto the waiting gurney and wheeled him inside the glass and aluminum entrance doors of the red-brick clinic.

"I'll have vitals for you in a sec," Abby said when they had moved Curly into the trauma room, a large, well-stocked room reserved for critical cases.

The serious knot on the side of his gray old head indicated the likely cause of his unconsciousness. But Maude wondered if he had fallen because he was unconscious or if he was unconscious because he had fallen. One of the slippery slopes of emergency medicine.

"Jimmy." Maude turned to the wide-eyed kid standing at the foot of the cart. "Did you see what happened?"

"No, ma'am, Dr. DeVane. Black Jaxx came around the barn lookin' proud like he a'ways does when he's thrown a rider. When I got to Granddad, he was on the ground."

"You should have let the rescue squad bring him in the ambulance."

"He'd'a killed me dead if I'd done that. Heck, he'll yell at me anyway." The boy rubbed the back of his thick neck.

"I know." Maude put a hand on Jimmy's arm. "He told Doc Avery he was too old to have a fuss made over him."

Jimmy grinned, then his face got serious again. "Will he wake up? Do you think you can save him, Dr. DeVane?"

"I'll know more after I examine him. If he wakes up soon, it'll be best."

Maude patted the old man's bony thigh through his worn jeans and started a more thorough exam. She gently prodded and searched for signs of injury, and just as she was satisfied there was no other neurological deficit, Curly began to mumble and tried to reach across his body with his left hand. Maude gently put his arm back at his side and let a little of her concern lift. Purposeful movement meant a decent level of brain function.

When Abby pulled off one boot, he murmured a few words.

Another moment later, "Danged horse," came out loud and clear, followed by something they probably didn't want to understand, period.

As Maude reached for Curly's right arm, he sat straight up. "What the hell's going on here?"

"Granddad!" Jimmy cried.

Curly looked around, blinked a few times and then swatted at Abby, who was tugging on his other low-heeled boot.

"And you can leave that right where it is, missy."

Abby easily evaded the swat and grinned at the old man. "Hullo, Curly Martin."

He let Abby ease him back against the pillow.

"Nurse Abby. Didn't expect to be back here so soon." With that, he gave Jimmy a look that made the boy squirm.

"I'm glad he brought you in, Mr. Martin." Maude put a hand on his shoulder to encourage him to stay put while she finished her exam.

Curly smirked his Montana charm and relaxed. "You're lookin' perty as a picture today, Maudie. But I guess it's Dr. DeVane nowadays."

"Well, Mr. Martin." Maude let the diminutive given to her in this valley when she was a child slide off her. "Now that you're smiling, you don't look so bad yourself. Does anything hurt?"

He grinned. "Just this." He held up the arm she had been about to examine. The bone under the brown weatherworn skin of his forearm jutted off in a slightly unnatural direction.

"Let me take a closer look at that," Maude said as she cradled his deformed wrist in the palm of her hand.

Curly's thick, frosty eyebrows drew together. "Nothin' a little time won't fix," he said as he tried to pull away.

"Curly Martin, are you in here giving people trouble again?"

All heads turned as the sound of the deep male voice thundered from the doorway. Maude smiled at her predecessor.

"Doc, I thought you left for civilization already." Curly grinned gap-toothed at Dr. William Avery, founder of the only clinic in her hometown, the place where Maude hoped to practice medicine as long as he had—hoped the town would let her.

"Don't you have a great-grandbaby back East to help birth?" Curly continued.

"Doc" pulled off distinguished-looking even in his travel clothes. "I heard you came all the way in from the ranch to say goodbye, so I stopped by for a minute." He gave Curly a cursory once-over, touching the bruise on Curly's head.

"Guess I wasn't glued on to that danged horse well enough."

"Good thing you landed on your hard head." Doc chuckled as he gently brushed a thumb over the wrist fracture.

"Dr. DeVane," he said as he turned to Maude, "I know you have everything under control here. If you have any questions, call me anytime."

"Thank you, I will. I hope you make it in time for the baby's birth, Dr. Avery." Maude smiled and kept her tone light. Doc Avery trusted her, but this visit would play differently through the gossip network. "Have a safe drive and a great retirement."

He smiled at her, patted Curly on the shoulder, nodded at Abby and Jimmy and walked out the door to his new life, no doubt leaving a trail of wagging tongues. *Old Doc Avery couldn't even get out of town without checking up on Dr. DeVane one last time. Lordy, what's going to happen to us when he's gone?*

Earlier at the grocery store she had overheard, "What if little Maudie messes up?" Did it not matter to anyone in this tiny throwback town that she had earned the M.D. after her name? She gave X-ray orders to Abby and left the room.

Well, she'd earn their trust. In the two years they had advertised for a doctor to take over the clinic, she was the only one to apply, and because she was their only choice of doctors in this valley, they'd have to give her what she needed to win them over—time.

TWELVE MOUNTAIN MILES northwest of St. Adelbert, on the Whispering Winds Ranch, where pine trees towered and snowcapped mountains etched the sky—the doorbell rang shrilly and repeatedly.

Guy Daley pushed away from the desk. Cynthia Stone, one of the participants in the executive development program, was at his door for the third day in a row with an excuse to chicken out of an activity. He had coerced her into the hike and the overnight, but this canyon crossing was going to be tricky.

The shrill bell rang again and he yanked the door open.

"Why's the door locked?" demanded the child on the stoop. She looked twenty, but he knew she was not quite thirteen. Mascara smeared under her eyes. Jeans shredded on the bottoms. Tail of her smudged pink T-shirt almost covering her belly and a riot of red curls mashed in on one side. She wore a deep scowl, just like her father had all those years ago when he'd run away from home and shown up at Guy's college apartment.

A fist of grief punched Guy in the gut. He took it and smiled at his niece.

"Lexic." He should be shocked or horrified she'd found her way, probably by herself, from Chicago to Montana, but he was oddly glad to see her.

"Uncle Guy." She glared at him, large blue eyes narrowed in challenge.

He reached for her bag, but she pulled away, so he stepped back to let her drag the purple duffle into the timbered living room. The last time he had tried to hug her, she'd slugged him.

"Does your mom know where you are?"

She shrugged one shoulder. "Kelly's too busy with the baby." She hefted the huge bag and hugged it to her. "Maybe she knows by now. I'm supposed to be at my friend's house until tomorrow."

Red streaks scored the whites of her eyes. "When was the last time you ate?"

She lifted the shoulder again.

Dirty, tired and hungry.

"Leave the bag. Go wash your hands."

She dropped the bag with a thud on the hardwood floor and headed down the hallway toward the bathroom.

"Eggs or cakers?" he called after her.

"Cakers." She turned for a moment and smiled sadly at him. Her father, his brother, had called pancakes "cakers," after a character in a kids' book. "And coffee."

"And orange juice," he muttered.

As she closed the bathroom door behind her, he took a second to feel the renewed ache spiraling through him. Maybe coming to his brother's ranch hadn't been such a good idea. Maybe he should have stayed in Chicago?

Twenty minutes later, Guy sat across the table and watched red curls bob up and down in rhythm to the forkfuls of pancakes being shoveled into the child's mouth.

"I called Kelly," Guy said of Lexie's stepmother. "She told me to tell you she's sorry you were unhappy."

She nodded and continued to fork in the fuel.

Her stepmother's exact words had been, "With the baby here I can't do this anymore. Keep her with you. Even I'm not uncaring enough to send her to your parents." Poor kid, if he was her last hope.

The whistle and choo-choo chugging of the ludicrous clock above the stove told him he was late for the start-up of this morning's executive training program. "Leap of Faith," Henry had named crossing a small canyon on a zip wire.

"I've got people to see. Will you be all right by yourself for a while?"

"I'm a kid, not an idiot." She forked in the last bite.

He smiled. So like her father.

She sat in front of the plate pooled with syrup, empty orange juice glass in her hand, and stared out the window at the sun-sprayed shadows in the pine trees behind the house.

"I wish I had more than a couple of years with him."

"I wish you did, too. Sleep might be a good idea right now. Your room is still there."

"I guess I could sleep a little." Her voice trembled as she spoke. She turned her big blue eyes, pooled with unshed tears, on him. "Kelly said you restarted Dad's business."

He gave her a grim nod. "Bessie and her daughter'll be back from shopping soon, so you won't be alone long."

She swiped the back of her hand at the tears and smiled. "I hope she got Twinkies."

He frowned.

"What? I already had two apples today. No, wait, that was yesterday, sometime." She did her shoulder thing. "I'll go up and sleep for a little while, and then you can tell me whether or not you're going to keep me."

"Lexie, this is your home anytime you want it to be."

"Yeah." She turned away.

Guy watched her bounce off as if she didn't have a care in the world. Her home. She'd had many in her short life.

"I'll be back by noon," he called after her.

UP ON A RIDGE a half mile away from the ranch house at the edge of a small canyon, Guy snugged the strap of the aerial-runway seat across Cynthia Stone's flabby abdomen.

"I don't want to be hurled across that damn canyon in this—this thing." Her voice scratched at his eardrums.

He crouched down beside her. "It'll be over soon."

"Let me out!" Little fat bulges stuck out here and there as she squirmed in her pale aqua warm-up suit.

"You won't go across unless you want to." He wasn't sure how his brother did this job, but right now it beat trying to practice medicine.

"Come on, Cynthia. Don't be a chicken. The fox won't bite," one of the executives called from the other side of the canyon.

"Fox? What fox? I wasn't told about any foxes." She jerked around to glare at Guy.

He checked a reply. He knew her well enough to know the "fox" distress was a delay tactic.

"An aerial-conveyance system like this is sometimes called a flying fox." Or death slide. "Aerial runway works for the purposes of Mountain High Executive Services. It's a kind of pathway from your old self to your new leader-conqueror self."

"My old self is just fine." She yanked on the harness. "How do I know this is safe?"

"Aircraft-grade wire." He pointed up to the wire above her head spanning the canyon. "Safety harness and a hand-activated braking system. You can't fall unless you try really hard, and you don't have to go fast." She'd be a piece of work on the high ropes tomorrow.

"What if it doesn't have one more crossing left in it?"

"Ms. Stone—"

She gave him a tired look, so he leaned in. "Cynthia—" He lowered his voice to just above a whisper.

She studied him as if seeing him for the first time.

"There are times when we have to take a leap, or we'll never know how far we can go." Guy tried to make the words sound sincere. He knew Henry would have.

"I didn't want to come here." Her tone was almost timid now. Apologizing. "My father made me."

"Where do you want to go in your company?"

"I'll be president and CEO one day."

"Because you're the owner's daughter."

She nodded.

"Is it enough for you to have the job because your blood

type is Stone, or do you want to be able to wield the authority you'll be given?"

When she didn't answer, Guy tugged hard on her harness to show her it was safe. "The others crossed. And some of them may deserve to be president or CEO one day. You only need to recognize that in yourself."

She grabbed the harness and held on for a ten-mile ride. Too bad she was only going a few hundred feet.

But, he might be getting through to her…

"Just shove me across the damn thing and get it over with. And that man at the other end had better catch me because I don't trust that flimsy-looking net, either."

Maybe not…

"Use the hand brake if you have to, but it's a gutsier experience if you let the net catch you."

"Just do it." She kicked up a puff of light brown dust.

Guy took hold of the harness and signaled Jake Hancock, the man who had been Henry's friend and right-hand man, and who now stood waiting at the other end of the runway.

"Are you sure?" he asked the woman in the harness.

She lifted her feet from the ground and glared at him.

He smiled and gave her a small push.

After a few seconds, she glided out over the rim of the canyon filled with jagged rocks and a few hardy plants. When she scanned the distance to the bottom, she let out a shriek so piercing Guy expected birds to fall from the sky.

"I got you, Ms. Stone," Jake shouted as he gestured to show her he was waiting on the far side to help her.

Hang in there a few more seconds, Guy thought as she picked up speed and hurtled toward the other side.

"Stop me! Stop—ME!" The closer she got to the end, the harder she kicked and squirmed.

"Use the hand brake, Ms. Stone," Guy called.

"Nooooo, I can't!" She began to flail her legs wildly.

As Jake reached out for her, she jerked backward and snapped her legs straight out; a blink later she landed with the thud of both feet in the middle of Jake's chest.

Guy watched in horror as Jake flew backward, landed, bounced and lay still in the dust. Guy grabbed a spare harness and attached it to the aerial runway.

"Get her off." He waved at the others as Cynthia sat sagging in the rig, her head resting against the safety netting.

Instead of assisting Cynthia, the other five executives rushed up to Jake's unmoving form.

"Cynthia, get out of the harness," Guy shouted.

After a few more moments of helpless watching, he broke one of Henry's cardinal safety rules and crossed the gap while Cynthia still hung in her harness.

When he reached the other side, he dug his boots in to stop near where Jake lay on the ground. "I'll be right back, Cynthia." He signaled to the still-dangling woman.

"He's breathing," a lithe forty-something executive said as she lifted her ear from Jake's chest. Guy was sure the woman had wanted to put her head on the rugged cowboy's chest since the first day.

Guy knelt beside the man on the ground and shook him gently. "Jake, open your eyes."

Jake blinked. "What?" He started to sit up.

A sharp scream came from over his shoulder. Guy turned to see Ms. Stone on the ground curled up in a ball.

He turned back to Jake. "Don't move until I can check you." He gave Jake a reassuring pat and addressed the woman who had had her ear on Jake's chest. "Stay with him." To which she nodded agreeably.

Guy ran to where Ms. Stone lay sprawled on the ground. What a sight, all that aqua covered with dust.

"My ankle. My ankle," she cried when she saw him, and then moaned loudly.

"Ms. Stone, it's all right. I'll help you."

"It's broken. I knew I shouldn't have done it. I knew it was wrong to come here." She waved a hand as if she were referring to all of Montana.

She probably was.

"Relax and let me have a look at your ankle."

"Don't touch me. I want a doctor, not a seminar leader."

It was the last thing he wanted to do, but he nodded. "I'll take you to the doctor."

He thought of the doctor in St. Adelbert, Dr. Maude DeVane. He should have let her take advantage of his younger brother's good nature and generous heart all those years ago.

He could have saved Henry from a gold digger.

IN TOWN, Curly Martin held up his hot-pink cast. "Thank you so much, Dr. DeVane. This ought to set their tongues a waggin'." He guffawed and stepped down from the table in the ortho room where he had acquiesced to sit so Maude could cast his arm properly.

"I'll walk you out, Curly," Maude said. Her suggestion of keeping Curly for observation had been met with true mirth by the nonagenarian. "What'll happen, Dr. DeVane?" he'd said. "I might die before my time?"

The phone on the main desk rang as Maude and Curly passed. Abby snatched it up and began to write on a notepad.

"Remember." Maude walked beside the old man. "If

there's a problem, I want to see you within the hour, not the next day because you decided to wait and see what happened."

"Told ya, did he."

"Jimmy did the right thing to bring you here. And I want to check your arm in two weeks."

"I'll be good, Dr. DeVane."

Curly's great-grandson, who had been banished to the truck for "showing a bit too much concern for such a young fella," jumped out and took his great-grandfather by his uninjured arm.

Curly turned back toward Maude and rolled his eyes, but he let the boy help him as if he needed it.

"Thanks a million, Doctor," Jimmy called over his shoulder as he stuffed Curly into the cab of the truck.

"Curly, either stay on the horse, or stay off it." Maude smiled at the old man.

He grinned and waved with the cast she had applied because she didn't think he'd keep a splint on for any longer than he was in her direct sight. The pink had been his idea.

As they drove off, an eddy of dust from their wake made its way across the town's wide main thoroughfare and dissipated against the white-and-blue facade of Alice's Diner. There had been many an "Alice" over the years. In the distance, a flock of birds flew above the trees with the sun glistening off the white of their feathers.

"Home." Contentment like she hadn't known in years swept through her. Soon, it wouldn't matter that she had once been the little girl everyone called Maudie.

As she reentered the building, Abby came toward her with a paper in her hand. "There's two more coming in,

Dr. DeVane. An ankle. Not too serious, by the sound of it. The other was kicked in the chest."

"Any details on the second one?" Kicked in the chest by a horse or a steer was often life threatening. Broken ribs. Punctured lungs. Bruised heart muscle. "Kicked by what?"

"They say he seems fine, but he was apparently kicked by the other one."

"Hard enough to hurt an ankle?" Maude gave a small shudder as she thought of how that might have come about. "How soon?"

"A few minutes. And there's one more thing."

"Yes?"

"They're coming from Mountain High."

"But—" Maude stopped as pain rushed in and nearly took her breath away.

"I'm sorry, Dr. DeVane. I know Henry was your friend."

"It's okay." Maude waved off the nurse's concern and turned into the office. Someone had restarted Henry Daley's business. When the young entrepreneur had died last summer, she had thought Mountain High Executive Services had died with him.

She sat down to enter notes in Curly's medical record, but tapped a pen tip on the clipboard instead. The first time she met Henry, he had tried to die on her. Before she got the chance to make a diagnosis, his arrogant, older, M.D. brother whisked the younger man away to another hospital.

Henry…

"Dr. DeVane?"

Maude cleared the tightness from her throat and faced Abby. "Are they here?"

"The van's coming up the street. Carolyn's still here and we'll call if there's something you need to see right away."

"Thanks, Abby," Maude said as Abby hurried away.

Maude repositioned the squeezy clip in the back of her wavy, shoulder-length brown hair. The clinic was old-fashioned in some respects, but the nurses, like Abby, and techs, like Carolyn, were as good as those at big-city clinics.

They had to be; they cared for their neighbors every day.

After a few minutes, the automatic doors opened, and a loud wail filled the clinic. Maude leaped from her chair and stepped out into the hallway to see Carolyn pushing a wheelchair filled with a mildly obese, fifty-something woman.

"Is that the doctor? Help me, Doctor." The woman reached toward Maude with outstretched hands.

Carolyn, a small woman with big red glasses, an X-ray technician by training and one of Doc Avery's long-standing assistants, patted the woman's shoulder. "Dr. DeVane will be in as soon as I get you more comfortable, ma'am."

The woman wailed again, and the tech hurried her off to a treatment room.

The outside doors whooshed open and Abby entered, pushing an empty wheelchair. The second patient walked beside her. When he saw Maude, the man touched a finger to the brim of an imaginary hat. "Hello, Dr. DeVane." Grief touched his look.

She led him toward the treatment room. "Mr. Hancock, I'll be in to see you after the nurse gets you settled." Jake had been the one who'd called her in Chicago about Henry's fatal accident, but true to his tacit nature, she got few details. Jake must have somehow restarted Mountain High.

Maude turned away and as she did, she noticed a man in the clinic doorway standing with his back to her. The glare of the bright sun pouring in the doorway outlined his tall form, his broad shoulders and trim waist, a man of her fantasies, if she ever had time for those anymore. The man lifted a folded piece of paper and tilted his head like—

"Guy Daley."

The name escaped as her heart began to pound. She forced a breath in and out…remembering.

In spite of the cold, his kiss had made her feel as if she were riding a wind on fire. Dangerous and exciting, it had left her soul scorched. But whatever she had thought she felt for this man, he had killed on that rainy Chicago night.

He stepped forward out of the halo of sunlight into the artificially lit hallway, dressed in ranch-work clothes, his challenging gaze fixed on her. She found herself staring into dark eyes. Eyes she once gazed into wondering if there were feelings for her buried somewhere in the deep shadows.

A primal urge arose in her, a craving she had wanted never again to have for this man. She crushed it.

*Fool me once…*

"Hello, Dr. Daley," she said, glad her voice came out strong and firm. So much for being the only doctor in the valley.

"Dr. DeVane."

"I'm sorry about your brother." She squared her shoulders as if he might fight her on her right to feel anything for Henry. He had in the past.

"Thank you," was all he said, but his expression slid to one with a chilling lack of emotion as he tucked the paper he had been reading into his shirt pocket.

"Are you here about the people from Mountain High?" She gestured down the hallway toward the treatment rooms.

"I am."

"Did Mr. Hancock restart the program?"

"No." The clipped response demanded no further questions.

But she ignored it. "Then who—"

"I would have thought you'd know I was on the ranch," he said before she had a chance to finish what she was about to ask.

The sharp tone of his words almost made her laugh. He had disliked her for so long it didn't bother her much anymore. And now that Henry was gone, she realized, it didn't have to bother her at all. "I'm the last stop on the gossip network."

A loud wail filled the hallway.

"Does this clinic have the facilities to see these patients or should I take them to a bigger town?"

She thought of her first week of emergency medicine rotation when the great Dr. Daley had yanked his younger brother from her care and taken him to another hospital.

"I'll see them and if you don't like what I have to say, Kalispell is about two hours away—each way—from the ranch."

She lifted her chin, but he said nothing.

Into the silence, the patient wailed again, this time holding the quavering tone like a coyote announcing territory.

"I have patients to see." She headed toward the keening.

"There's nothing wrong with her ankle." His voice was a low rumble behind her.

"I get to decide that," she said without turning.

As she walked toward the room, she found herself wondering why the highest and mightiest emergency medicine physician in the Midwest was tucked away on a ranch in Montana.

"Hello. I'm Dr. DeVane," Maude said as she pushed back the curtain in the room where the woman sat with one foot elevated on a pillow.

Ms. Stone greeted her and then shifted to fidget with the bright white sheet the way one might expect a nervous queen on her throne to tend the folds of her velvet gown.

"Tell me what happened, Ms. Stone."

"What happened is that seminar leader made me break my ankle." She put her head back and her arm over her face.

Seminar leader? She called Dr. Guy Daley a seminar leader?

"Let me take a look at your ankle, and then you can tell me how you were injured."

Maude lifted the sheet and the ice pack to see a pale, puffy ankle.

"It all started…"

*It all started* was usually not a good place to begin.

"…when my father—"

"Why don't we start with when you injured your ankle?"

After listening and examining, Maude had to agree. Guy Daley's assessment was probably correct. There was no injury, but in case there was some unseen problem, she gave the patient the benefit of the doubt. "We'll get some X-rays."

"Thank you so much, Doctor."

The long, low moan the woman gave out this time had Maude biting her lip and hurrying out the door, grateful she had somewhere else to be. Abby should have a set of vitals and a brief history from Jake by now.

"Really? X-rays?" Guy Daley put out his hands to fend her off as she nearly plowed into him.

She sidestepped and exhaled a huff of air to short circuit the emotions her brain was trying to make from the smell of clean cotton and male pheromones. "This clinic may be in the back woods, but we treat the patient's privacy as a serious matter."

"Don't let that seminar leader tell you what to do, Doctor," Ms. Stone called from the treatment room.

Guy pulled her away from the doorway.

She frowned down at where he held her arm and then up into his face. His dark gaze challenged her and then he let go. "I suspect Ms. Stone is looking for sympathy."

"If she's not injured, why did you bring her here?"

"She wanted to see a doctor. Jake and Bessie are the only people out here that know I'm a physician—and you."

The level gaze he aimed at her told Maude he wasn't about to expound. This time she didn't challenge him.

"You can have a seat—" she started.

"—in the waiting room? No, thank you. I'll be back after I see to a few things." He immediately walked toward the exit. The arrogance that should have been in his step was missing.

She wondered if he had secrets as desperate as her own.

"Dr. DeVane?"

Maude turned as the nurse approached her. "Yes, Abby."

"You might want to come right away."

# CHAPTER TWO

GUY SLIPPED OUT into the warming wind of the early afternoon. He had seen the questions in Maude DeVane's eyes, and he had no intention of sharing his grief with someone whose loss could be measured in dollars. He kicked a pebble with the toe of his boot and stepped off the curb to cross the wide street.

He remembered the feel of her responsive lips beneath his. Five years ago, for one brief moment he had wanted to be wrong about her. He rubbed the back of his hand across his mouth. He wouldn't be surprised if Maude DeVane still held out hope that Henry had somehow left the ranch that had been her parents' to her.

As he reached the far side of the street, he stopped in front of the diner and slid the letter that had arrived in this morning's mail from his pocket.

*To Whom It May Concern*: the letter began. Kelly was right about his parents. This letter was from their attorney, most likely at his mother's behest. *Any and all persons now occupying the Whispering Winds Ranch shall vacate...*

*Nice bluff, Mother.* His parents had no control over Lexie's inheritance, but that didn't stop them from trying. As the firstborn son, Guy had been the only focus of their attention. Everything he did mattered. Everything Henry did was irrelevant. Guy had tried to shield Henry as much as he could, but Henry was only eight when Guy went off to college. After Guy left, Henry accelerated his campaign to get their parents to notice him. By the time Henry got out of high school, he had already begun a series of extreme adventure trips that would ultimately take his life.

Now Lexie's grandparents wanted control of the ranch. If Guy thought for a moment they had forgiven Henry for fathering a child at age fifteen with a casual acquaintance, he might think they were trying to protect Lexie. He knew his parents well enough. If there was wealth they could control, they thought it some sort of negligence not to try.

Guy tossed the letter into a nearby trash can, and headed down the block. "Stop at the hardware store," was Bessie's plea to anyone from the ranch who went to town. There was always something at the cluttered, dusty old store the ranch needed.

"Hello, Mr. Daley." The storeowner smiled at Guy and furrowed his well-trimmed eyebrows. "Bessie called. Said she didn't have lightbulbs on her list this morning and she'd appreciate if you'd get some. Also says she wishes you'd carry your phone."

"Thanks." Guy gave the storekeeper what he hoped was an equally friendly Montana-like smile. At the lightbulb display, he touched where the pocket of his lab coat would have been and where his cell phone and pager had spent most of his waking hours. No lab coat. No cell phone. No hospital pager.

He bowed his head and studied blue-and-yellow lightbulb packages before he chose several with no dust.

At the checkout, he picked up a handful of Tootsie Pops in a bouquetlike arrangement and laid it on the counter beside the lightbulbs. He thought about it for moment, and added a second colorful bouquet.

MAUDE PUSHED OPEN the treatment-room door to see Jake Hancock perched on the edge of the patient cart, hospital gown draped loosely over his torso. As Maude stepped inside the room, Abby took up a position at the door, as if she might tackle him if he tried to leave. And she might.

"Abby says you're trying to bolt."

"The longer I sit here, the sillier I feel, ma'am."

"Tell me what happened to you."

"Nothing worth frettin' about."

Maude took a step closer. "Well, now that you're already here, I'll examine you, take a listen to your chest and if need be, we'll go from there."

"Is it really necessary?" He swung one leg and tapped the cart's metal end with a boot heel.

She stared steadily at him and knit her eyebrows as if contemplating a great puzzle. She knew his type. Needed a limb dangling before help seemed necessary. "That's one of the tricky things about trauma medicine. Sometimes I don't know if it's 'necessary' until I examine the patient and see if it's necessary."

"You're sure?"

"There is one tried-and-true way to cover the worst-case scenario without examining you." She reached into her pocket and pulled out a small tag with a string attached to it by way of a reinforced hole. One of the M.D.'s who'd helped her train in rural medicine had given it to her. *One of my old tricks,* he had said.

Maude had thought she'd never use it, but here she was handing it to her third patient.

Abby laughed out loud and came up to stand beside Jake.

Jake took the small tag and let it dangle from his fingertips. "What's this?"

"A toe tag." Abby doubled over as she spoke.

Maude held a steady, serious expression. "Tie it on your big toe. Saves us the trouble if…"

Jake held up a hand to stop her. "You're very persuasive, Dr. DeVane."

"It's how I can afford my yacht." She took the tag from him and tucked it back into her pocket.

He looked at her briefly and then laughed. "Trying to picture someone tugging a yacht up into these mountains."

She took the stethoscope from her pocket and held it in her hands. "So, tell me how you feel."

He settled back as if he might stay for the exam. "Like I was kicked into the dirt by a Boardroom Betty. Mostly a pride injury, I suspect. I was only down for a couple seconds."

"He has two small impact marks on his chest," Abby offered.

Maude examined him, read the electrocardiogram and found nothing to make her think he had any serious side effects from the kick or the fall, but harbored her usual suspicion for a posttrauma case.

"Sir, you seem to have pronounced your diagnosis correctly. You are 'fine' as far as your exam and tests show."

He leaped off the cart and grabbed the blue work shirt from the counter.

"We'll give you privacy to dress, but don't leave yet."

"Yes, ma'am. And, please, tell the boss I didn't just get up and run away. He's likely not to believe me." He smiled at them as Maude and Abby stepped into the corridor.

"I'll tell him, Mr. Hancock." Maude pulled the door closed.

Now, back to the seminar leader's problem pupil.

Seminar leader. It's not that she hated Guy Daley or anything—not really. He was being a big brother looking after Henry. Though he was overbearing and a snob and sometimes...

Maybe she hated him a little. She'd have to work on that one if they were going to live in the same valley. Henry had loved him after all. Maybe he'd mellowed in the years since she'd seen him.

"Excuse me." Guy stood in the hallway, his hair a bit disheveled. A dark lock fell over his forehead, making him look a little like a cross between a certain superhero and his alter ego.

Feelings shot through her which she banished almost before she acknowledged them.

"The tech has the X-rays finished. They look... Well, they're ready for you to read," he said, as he followed her down the hallway.

She stopped and turned. "Dr. Daley."

"I'll be waiting down there." He gestured toward the entrance and walked away.

She smiled a little. He couldn't stand to be sent to the waiting room instead of doing the sending.

She continued to the small recess that served as the tiny clinic's supply closet and X-ray viewing room. The tech had kindly moved the mop and pail out of the way so she could get a good close look at the X-ray films.

A few minutes later, she went in to see Ms. Stone and found her patient reclined on the cart with a damp washcloth over her eyes. Maude touched the woman's arm.

"Yes." Cynthia's voice was weak and, well, pathetic if Maude was to go there.

"Ms. Stone, I've looked at your X-rays."

The patient removed the cloth from her eyes. A hopeful look spread over her face. Maude liked giving good news. It was one of the best parts of being a doctor.

"There's no break and no signs of any degenerative joint disease. The bone structure of your foot and ankle looks just fine."

Ms. Stone's expression became distorted. But she remained silent.

Not exactly the reaction Maude expected.

"You might have a small muscle tear or a strained ligament which wouldn't show up on X-ray. The tech will tell you what you need to do for it, give you home-care instructions and wrap it with an elastic bandage. If it hurts too much, use an over-the-counter pain medication. I'll call—"

Ms. Stone began to squirm and look around the room, to look anywhere except at Maude.

"Is there something wrong?" Maude asked.

"I can't go with Mr. Daley. You'll have to keep me here until I'm better." She still avoided looking at Maude.

"Is there a problem I should know about?" Other than a problem with a hotshot emergency doctor not telling anyone he was a physician? Maude quickly put the thought away. She could examine it when she had no one else's welfare at stake.

"I can't go back to that place." Ms. Stone studied her chipped nail polish intently.

"I'm sorry. We have no overnight facilities at the clinic."

"I need to stay here until I can travel," she said after a few more moments of polish-studying.

"There are motels nearby."

The woman looked away, and when she looked back, there were tears in her eyes.

"Then I'd—" She paused.

"Yes?" Maude placed a hand on her patient's shoulder.

"I'd be alone."

Maude wondered if Cynthia Stone had ever been alone. She'd met the type, always had nannies, traveling companions, live-in servants. Never alone.

"You wouldn't be by yourself at the ranch. It's such a pretty place."

"You know it? You know that place and about that thing he has strung across the canyon?"

Maude smiled. She hadn't seen Henry's contraptions, but he had an uncanny respect for the land; she trusted him to somehow make Mountain High fit in to the natural surroundings.

She realized Ms. Stone was waiting for a response.

"You chose to participate in the program, didn't you?"

"Well—um—yes."

"And you paid for it?"

"Of course." She looked at her fingernails again. "Well, my father did."

Maude stepped back and folded her arms over her chest. "Then you're the boss. Choose to participate or choose not to. They can't make you do anything you don't want to do. You can discuss options with the people from Mountain High."

Cynthia Stone crossed her arms over her chest, mimicking Maude's stance, but said nothing.

"I'll send in D—um—Mr. Daley." Mr. Daley. Dr. Daley, whatever. It wasn't her place to rat him out.

Cynthia huffed out a derisive sound. "It won't do any good. I don't trust any of them. I don't know what they think they're doing out there in the middle of the wilderness on that horrible ranch."

"I'll send him in."

Maude left the door slightly ajar as she exited the room. Horrible ranch. She thought many things of the ranch where she grew up, but horrible was never one of them. Not even when its isolation helped cause great harm to her sister.

She remembered the ever-present smile on the face of her beautiful sister. A sister who had once been so smart and capable.

"You can go in and see Ms. Stone now," Maude said as she approached Guy Daley. "She's convinced she needs to stay."

He nodded and disappeared into the treatment room.

If he didn't talk the woman into leaving, there was always Sheriff Potts. The imposing man with the badge had little trouble in a face-to-face confrontation. Though law enforcement was rarely needed in the small rural valley's only clinic, the sheriff was always glad to help out—at least that's what Doc Avery told her. He had told her a lot of things during the short two weeks she had to get acquainted with his, and now her, practice.

Not much later, Maude looked up from the office desk where she was finishing paperwork to see Guy coming down the hallway toward her. So soon. She wondered if she'd need the sheriff after all.

"The tech is helping her learn how to use crutches and then I'll take her back to the ranch."

Maude swallowed a startled "What?" She couldn't

believe the woman in the treatment room would consent to going anywhere with him, let alone back to the ranch, and so quickly.

"She said she'd leave because—" He paused.

She checked to see if he was gloating.

Holding his expression emotionless, he said, "I told her you'd make a house call."

She pushed up from her chair to face him. "You what? A house call? For a minor ankle injury?" She thought of the old and the infirm patients Doc Avery used to visit at home. She would gladly see those people, but Cynthia Stone didn't fit any category of patient who might need a house call.

"Having you come by to check up on her was the only thing that got her interested in leaving."

The ranch. The place she had managed, with one excuse or another, not to go back to for over ten years.

"Tell her I won't be there."

"She's your patient," he stated matter-of-factly, and walked out the door.

Even after Henry most generously bought the ranch from her parents to save them from bankruptcy and to fund their retirement and her sister's care—Maude could not make herself return.

Soon, Mountain High's blue van pulled up to the door.

Yes, she did hate Guy Daley. She did so want to be bigger than that, but he made it too easy.

Worse—

He was forcing her hand. She should visit the ranch for her own sake. She hadn't had the moral fortitude to go back there since she left for medical school, and had even less courage after her parents sold the ranch to Henry. Making a house call would keep her from chickening out.

She stepped into the warm afternoon sunlight and walked over to where Guy stood looking tall and Western, not at all like a Chicago doctor, and leaning on the van's driver's side door with his arms crossed.

"I'll come," she said as she stopped in front of him.

He unfolded his arms and looked at her to continue.

"Please keep an eye on Mr. Hancock. My confidence is low that he'd report any problems if he had them."

Guy frowned and Maude knew he wanted to ask for confidential patient information, but he didn't, always the utmost professional. Recalling the earlier promise she'd made, she said, "He asked that I tell you he 'didn't just get up and run away.' That I released him."

"That would be Jake." One corner of his mouth turned up into the beginnings of what she knew to be a beguiling smile.

Oh, yes. This was Henry Daley's brother. Charm had poured from Henry at every turn. From his brother it had to be coaxed and, if given, was hard fought for. The only people she ever saw charm the great Dr. Daley were his brother Henry and Henry's daughter, Lexie. For Maude, the charm had never been there.

"I'll come tomorrow morning." "Solo practice" popped into her head. "Make that afternoon. Tuesday morning is office hours, there are patients for me to see."

"Tomorrow afternoon then."

She could have sworn he gave her the tiniest of bows before he reached for the sliding passenger door and made himself busy making room for Queen Cynthia.

As Maude turned away, a sense of relief flooded through her, followed quickly by annoyance. She couldn't let Guy

Daley get to her. Much water had flowed under many bridges for both of them, and the past needed to stay in the past.

THE NEXT MORNING, dressed in her neatly pressed blue oxford shirt and navy slacks with her lab coat over her arm, Maude entered the foyer of the Wm. Avery Clinic ready to let people see how well she could do the job. The truth be told, she was better than old Doc Avery, at least technically, and the more patients she kept alive and healthy, the more people in this valley would accept her as Dr. DeVane and forget about little Maudie.

Arlene, the receptionist, looked up with a nervous smile. That would change, Maude knew. They'd all get used to her.

"Good morning, Arlene." Maude turned slowly in the empty reception area. "Are they all in the treatment rooms?"

"I'm sorry, Dr. DeVane." The receptionist took the pencil from behind her ear and fiddled with it. "They—um—canceled and two of them who are usually early didn't show up at all. I'm really sorry. Mrs. Effington was here for her nine-thirty, but when she saw no one else was here, she—um—decided to leave, too."

"Is there anyone left on the books for today?"

"Only Mr. Stanley to have his stitches taken out, and he's already in one of the exam rooms."

Maude felt some of the puff go out of her ego, but she was careful not to let Arlene see. "And he's only here because he can't take the stitches out himself?"

"I suspect you're right, Dr. DeVane. Can I get you a

cup of coffee, or maybe tea?" Arlene was trying hard to put her at ease.

"No, thank you. Say, Arlene, how would you like a paid day off?" The offer didn't seem to make Arlene any more comfortable and Maude continued. "I'll see Mr. Stanley and while I do, you make a note for the door. If anyone needs us, they can call the emergency number, and you won't have to be here all morning without anyone to greet."

"I can do paperwork."

"Paperwork will keep." Maude gestured at the empty waiting room. "They'll come back. In the meantime, we'll make lemonade out of this big lemon of a day."

Arlene nodded and Maude went in to see the only one of Dr. Avery's patients willing to have her treat him this morning.

After Arlene left, Maude stayed at the office for a while. When she was tired of reading charts, but mostly frustrated at being alone, she went to find an ear that would give her sympathy—or a knock upside the head, whichever she needed the most.

"SALLY, THEY STOOD ME UP!" Maude said as she entered the back door of a large, rambling old house in a cul-de-sac only a few blocks from her own tidy little home.

Sally Sanderson, Maude's friend since childhood, glanced up from the washer into which she had been shoving colorful clothing of many small sizes. "Well, I'm glad."

"What?"

Sally snorted a laugh as she pulled her mop of blond curls away from her gray eyes and pushed her glasses up on her nose. "Go pour us some coffee. I'll be done in a sec."

Maude put cream and sugar into Sally's—*I need the energy,* she had said about the added calories—and sat down to wait. Sally did need the energy. Her slight five-foot-two-inch body chased five children all day and half the night.

"I wasn't sure I'd get to see much of you after Doc left," Sally said as she set a basket of folded towels by the door and took a seat at the worn wooden table big enough to seat the small army of Sandersons and a few more.

"Me, too." Maude laughed. "Doc Avery was supposed to be here for a month after I got here, but it seems their granddaughter had her delivery date recalculated."

"Mommy. Mommy."

Sally reached down and picked up Lizzy, a shy five-year-old replica of herself, who had wandered into the room, spotted the intruder and made a beeline for the safety of her mother's lap. The sparkling stars mounted on floppy stalks attached to the headband Lizzy wore batted her mother on the chin and Sally pushed them gently aside. "Doc's gone only one day and here we are. I'm delighted to have your company."

"I'm glad you are. Thank you."

"All right. So what's that about?" Sally stroked Lizzy's hair.

"Yesterday morning at the grocery store they were gossiping, called me little Maudie."

"And you just had to hide behind the dill pickle display and listen?"

"Well something like that. It was canned peas." Maude reached down and patted Barney, the docile family dog that had followed Lizzy into the room and now sat with his head against Maude's leg. "What if this keeps up?"

Sally snort-laughed again and Lizzy looked up at her. "This is St. Adelbert, honey. It took them a year to decide to plant flowers around the flagpole in the town square. Give them time."

"I just feel sort of blindsided. I came here because I knew there would be no one when Doc Avery left. It's not as if I'm an outsider. They know me. Most of them know my family. Was I some kind of moron when I was a child?"

"No, but you were cute." Sally hugged the child on her lap. Laughter played in her big wide-set eyes.

"Cute? Who wants a cute doctor?" Maude stirred her coffee.

"Barry Farmington."

"Oh, please. He doesn't count. He'd hit on a lamppost if he thought he could get some." Maude sipped coffee, put it down and stirred again.

"They'll come around," Sally assured her.

"What do I do in the meantime? I'm used to working sixteen hours a day." Maude tapped her fingertips on the tabletop until Sally reached over and quieted the tapping by covering Maude's hand with her own.

"Since it won't last long, take some time for yourself. Drive to Kalispell and have a massage. Go out and make new friends. Eat dirt. What do you feel like doing?"

"I don't know. Yesterday, when a patient came in as an emergency, someone must have called Doc Avery. He stopped in…on his way out of town."

"Cora and Ethel. Know everything. Blab all." Sally smoothed the hair back from her daughter's forehead. Lizzy snuggled closer into her mother's bosom.

"You heard." Maude crossed and uncrossed her legs.

Sally nodded. "I was behind the cornflakes this morning."

Maude put her face in her hands.

"It's early." Sally patted her on the head and played with her hair the way she did her daughter's. "Besides, they asked you to come and take over."

Maude laughed and looked up. "I didn't tell you what they said the first time I called, when I was just starting my Rural Medicine fellowship. It's too embarrassing."

"How about…'Oh, Maudie, you're too cute to be our doctor'?"

"Close. 'We're sure we'll find someone before you're ready.' I know I heard the head of the selection committee cringe when she said it, too, hoping I wasn't going to beg for crumbs or anything. That was two years ago and I was already board certified in internal medicine."

"The jerks, but like I said…"

"I know. It's early." Maude sat up and pulled her shoulders back, and then slumped forward onto her elbows. "Maybe I'll go to Fiji and then come back next spring to see if 'little Maudie' is better than no doctor at all."

"Yeah, go. And while you're there, you can choose another profession, maybe something that doesn't take any backbone."

As if to emphasize Sally's point, Barney put his paws on Maude's lap and stretched up to lick her face. "Thank you. I needed that," she said to Sally and Barney. She scratched the back of the dog's head.

"See the patients that come. Treat them like kings and queens, and give away ice-cream cones. They'll come back."

"Possibly. Where are the rest of the kids?" Maude reached out and touched the silken cheek of the girl in her friend's lap and got a shy smile as a reward.

"The twins are having a nap—early, but I take what I can get. The older two are on a playdate, so I have peace and quiet—just what you're shunning. Remember this day. You'll rue it if you waste it. Now tell me what else has you going."

"Going?"

"You're twitchy and I know all this maudlin—" she paused to cover Lizzy's ears "—crap is a cover-up for what you don't want to talk about."

"I am not—" Maude gestured with her spoon "—twitchy."

"You stirred your black coffee. Twice. The only time you get that twitchy is when— Oh, yes." Sally threw a fist in the air. "Lizzy honey, Mommy wants you to take that pack of Oreos we just bought and go watch television."

Maude dropped her coffee spoon on the table with a clatter. She eyed her friend suspiciously as Lizzy hopped down, sprinted for the cupboard and, hardly stopping, turned and ran to the family room holding her prize with both hands, blond curls flying, sparkling stars dancing wildly.

"A whole pack of cookies *and* television?"

"Who is he?"

"No. No. No." Maude held her hands up. "It's not what you think. He isn't anyone."

"Better and better. You usually fall for the somebodies who treat you badly and send you back crying to me."

"I don't cry. Besides, I like to think I dump them. I'm a busy doctor, remember. No time for such dalliances. Love 'em and leave 'em."

"Let's see. It's not Curly or Jimmy Martin. Who else did

you see yesterday? Um. Oh, yes, Jake, but he's not your type. He's the right age and heaven knows good looking."

"Hey, Jake Hancock's an idea." Maude knew where Sally was heading, and she didn't want to go there.

"Is not. He's too cowboy for you. Besides, if you'd have thought so, you'd have jumped his bones when your parents tried to set you up with him a couple years ago, after they moved off the ranch."

"And they had nothing left to do but meddle in their daughter's life," Maude finished for her.

Sally tapped her chin. "There's a man out at your ranch running Mountain High. It must be him."

"It isn't and never has been *my* ranch."

"Oh, you are dodging on this one. He was in town a couple of times before you got here. I hear he's hunky."

"Sally, he's Henry's brother," Maude said.

"The doctor? From Chicago?" Sally folded her arms over her chest and wrinkled her brow. "We don't like him, do we?"

"I'm trying not to hate him." Maude let a flash of pain for her lost friend Henry grip her.

"Just give me ten minutes with the man."

Maude laughed imagining five-foot-nothing Sally taking on Guy Daley. She'd do it, too.

"What's he doing on your ranch, anyway?"

Maude started to reply, but Sally waved her off. "I know you don't own it, but you should."

"Because I grew up there?"

Sally nodded emphatically.

"The truth is—" Maude paused.

"What? What have you been hiding from me?"

Maude put her chin down toward her chest and then confessed, "I could have had it."

"The ranch!"

She nodded. "If I had wanted to be in debt until I was a hundred and ninety-three. The bank said as an M.D. and as a prospective long-standing member of the community we could work something out."

"So that's not it."

"No, it's not. I just couldn't imagine working that hard for something…" Maude let her voice trail off. She didn't know if she could say the words even to Sally. She barely said them to herself. She put her hands down on the table and rested her chin on them.

"Something?" Sally prodded in a gentle tone.

When Maude said nothing, Sally poked her on the arm. When Maude still didn't respond, Sally poked harder.

"Ouch." Maude rubbed her arm that really didn't hurt.

Sally had squared her shoulders and made herself look like Atlas ready to shoulder the world.

Maude chuckled. "Yeah, you don't have any worries of your own."

Sally relaxed against the slat-back chair. "Well, there is the new worry I have about Lizzy hurling Oreos all over the carpet in front of the TV because she's no doubt sitting too close, catching as much electromagnetic radiation as she can."

"Maybe we should go rescue her."

"Lizzy, sit on the couch and watch TV," Sally called over the sound of Big Bird. Then she looked at Maude and smiled. "I can always flip the couch cushion over. Now what's up with the ranch and how much does it have to do with one Daley brother or the other?"

"It didn't have anything to do with a Daley brother. At least it didn't at the time."

"It had to do with…" Sally peered over the top of her glasses at Maude.

"I didn't want to work that hard for something that broke my heart every day." Maude expelled a breath of frustration.

"Amanda," Sally said quietly.

Maude nodded her head as she thought of the accident twenty years ago that now seemed as if it had happened yesterday. "One day I was the goofy girl with an older sister who wanted to take over from Doc Avery and the next day all I had were neighbors hovering over me not telling me a thing about what was going on."

"And all this time, I thought it was because you couldn't afford it."

"Mom and Dad owed so much to the banks, I told them to sell it to the highest bidder."

"Yeah, one of those rich Coasters or some Arab sheik. I hate it when families move off the ranches."

"Henry was sanctimonious when he thought I'd lose my childhood home forever. He was determined I'd want it someday, so he bought it to save it from your Coasters and sheiks. Said he'd sell it to me when I was ready. He was so excited, I just couldn't convince him I might never want the ranch. And my parents, well, they were tickled to be out from under the burden and retire to Great Falls with the nest egg Henry overpaid them. And we all knew with Amanda in a bigger town, she'd be well taken care of for the rest of her life."

Sally rubbed Maude's shoulder. "Do you want the ranch now?"

"I don't. Too many memories. Too much work." But as she said the words she thought of taking a dip in the swimming hole and long hikes to the hunter's cabin.

"Are you sure?"

"We did have fun there."

The two friends sipped coffee as warm sunshine streamed between the white curtains with embroidered red tulips and fell over them like a warm blanket. Maude thought of the solace they had found in each other in grade school when they realized they each had an older sister who outshined them by, Sally had said, *about a gagillion candlepower.*

"Maudie likes the enemy," Sally singsonged softly.

"Creep." Maude laughed and smacked the top of the table with her hand. "I'm going back to the office where there is no one to tease me."

"No, you aren't. You're going to the hunk's ranch to make a house call."

"Nothing is a secret in this town."

"There's nine hundred and seventy-three of us in the entire valley besides you—no, nine hundred and seventy-four—Midge had her baby last week and, of course, we all know as much of everybody's business as we can ferret out or make up."

"Can we change the subject to something that doesn't involve me?"

"But you came here to talk about you."

"I came here to sulk. You can imagine the jubilation that will break loose in this town if they find out there is a real doctor, a man doctor, in the valley."

Sally waggled her blond eyebrows at Maude. "Want to eat Oreos and watch *Sesame Street?*"

"Yes, and then I have a house call to make."

Lizzy sat between them on the couch. All three wore headbands with sparkling stars on floppy stalks and ate cookies with a big yellow bird. Barney sat on the floor with his muzzle on the edge of the couch, eyes watching each cookie go from package to mouth, hoping.

EARLY WILDFLOWERS greeted Maude as she drove the highway toward the ranch. At intervals a granite gray stream rollicked beside the road, and in some places rough escarpments soared high, held back by luck and prayers.

Around many curves in the road, snowcapped mountains peeked above pine trees but never seemed to get any closer. Around others lay breathtaking drop-offs where the world fell away and if you drove off the edge, no one would find you for weeks—or ever.

Maude accelerated, loving the sense of adventure clinging to the edge gave her. She smiled. Henry had taught her to push the envelope once in a while. And then she slowed, wondering if anyone would ever care that she felt that way, if she'd ever have a relationship and a family like Sally had, if the town would ever accept her as their doctor.

What would her sister have done under the circumstances?

She gripped the steering wheel hard and then made herself relax. There wouldn't have been any such "circumstances." Amanda, the golden child, had been smart and beautiful with an aura of grace and strength. Everyone would have welcomed her warmly as a replacement for Doc Avery…even though she wasn't a man.

She rounded the last sharp curve, and the valley green

with both darkness and light spread out before her. The stunning nature of the land had not changed.

She could face Guy Daley—

"Oh God." She laughed. She had tried so hard not to think of him. If what didn't kill you made you stronger, then this man had contributed greatly to her strength over the years.

She slowed to turn onto the long road from the highway to the ranch house. The roughly graded gravel took her through what had been pastureland, but now seemed unused and undisturbed, still beautiful, not lessened by having nature's free hand.

As she rounded the last corner, the ranch house and buildings came into view.

She stopped near the barn.

A rustic yet sturdy-looking two-story log building stood next to the house, apparently a guesthouse for the participants in Henry's program. It didn't destroy the look of the homestead, but it had replaced the old oak tree. The one that Granddad had always insisted shouldn't be growing there, and maybe it shouldn't have been.

They'd put the building right where Amanda had lain for so long in the snow. A heart-wringing longing filled Maude, and she rested her forehead on her white-knuckled hands. She missed her sister and the life they'd had.

She suddenly felt closer to Amanda than she had in years. "I'm doing it, Amanda." She would fulfill her sister's dream no matter how hard she had to fight to get the people of the valley to accept her. The lovely, craggy valley, full of skeptical people, would have a doctor, one who cared, and one everyone could call Doc.

The sound of rapping on the window of the car brought her head sharply up.

# CHAPTER THREE

STANDING BESIDE Maude's car door, his dark hair glistening in the sunlight, planes of his chest distinct beneath the well-washed denim of his shirt, Guy Daley stared in at her. Shadows softened the contours of his face, and what he might be under his stern exterior caught her off guard.

She turned away as if to check the stack of papers on the seat beside her. When she turned back, the sun lit the true man. Shuttered, unreadable.

Showdown time. She could either back up and run him over or she could get out of the car and make nice with the man who always made it so possible for her to dislike him.

Dr. DeVane would make nice. She got out and kept the door between them. "Hello, how's Jake today?"

He nodded a greeting. "Annoyed."

"That doesn't seem like Jake." Irritability. A symptom of a problem she had not detected?

"He's been tending to Ms. Stone."

"Ah." She lifted her chin once in understanding. "I would guess she hasn't let up on her demands."

"You'd be right."

A small bell tinkled in the distance, and a moment later, Jake stepped out of the barn. His typically erect posture seemed a bit droopy today as he waved to her and headed toward the log guesthouse.

Maude covered her smile with her hand and when she regained control, she called to Jake as he mounted the porch. "I'll get that. If it's all right with you."

Only the perking up of Jake's posture let his relief show. "Thanks, Dr. DeVane. I expect she'll enjoy seeing someone besides me," he said, oh so politely, with a salute on his hat bill. He stepped off the porch and walked calmly into the barn where she suspected he locked and barred the door behind him.

"You've won over one cowboy," Guy said, his voice a low rumble no one would overhear but that murmured a warming frequency through her.

"Well, I've got a bell to answer." She tugged on her jacket and mentally stilled the useless humming inside her.

Guy stepped back only enough for her to pass. "She's on the second floor at the end of the hallway."

Maude nonchalantly edged between her car door and the man. The seductive smell of male-at-work filled her head, and the humming turned to heat until she thought she'd just take all her clothes off and demand satisfaction.

She gazed steadily into his face, refusing to let him see he had gotten to her in any way. "I'll find her."

"Follow the sound of the bell."

She thought his eyes twinkled, but twinkling like a star was not Guy Daley's way.

On the first floor of the guesthouse, where it smelled of wood and polish, she knew she stood where the tree had borne witness to the tragedy that had unfolded beneath its branches.

The tinkling bell hushed the memories and Maude ascended the stairs. In a sparsely but tastefully decorated room, Ms. Stone sat in a chair by the window. Her foot propped up on an ottoman, she looked as if she were holding court.

Maude examined her ankle and reconfirmed her diagnosis. They spoke about the next few days, when the group of executives was expected to depart the ranch.

"You can begin walking without the crutches now," Maude told her. "And if you're comfortable, you don't even need the Ace bandage."

"I'm so grateful there is a Chicago doctor all the way out here. Thank you for coming."

Wow, something in Cynthia Stone had changed, Maude thought as she left the room. She wondered what would happen if Ms. Stone knew there were two Chicago doctors all the way out here.

As Maude descended the stairs, she paused on the landing to appreciate the beauty of the ranch. Just then, Guy stepped from the barn and lifted his eyes to hers in a penetrating stare. Her heart rate sped up. She felt silly. He didn't even like her, for God's sake.

When she stepped out of the guesthouse, Guy was on the porch leaning on the rail looking even more cowboy. Her first impulse was to step close, inhale the smell of him and kiss him.

She checked that stuff right soon, but probably not before she gaped at him as if she were staring at Michelangelo's David for the first time.

It was a good thing he couldn't read minds. *Think of something else. Hunger.* "Ms. Stone seems content." She looked at her watch, really hungry. "And I have to go."

"Have you had lunch?"

"Um." Oh, she hoped he didn't read the rest of the stuff inside her head. "If having Oreo cookies counts."

"When I told Bessie you were coming to see Ms. Stone, she left a spread. A thank-you, I suppose. And then they all went shopping."

The thrum of his voice sent a wave of sizzling energy through her, and she had to give herself a mental swat.

"I wasn't really planning on staying." No lunch. No tour. No lusting after the enemy. No long goodbye to the ranch.

She inhaled a deep breath, and her head filled with pine-scented memories. Oak tree gone, new guesthouse, Guy Daley…the swimming hole, the rich, tall forest, beautifully clean air, lazy summer mornings… She wanted to take one of those new guest rooms and stay forever.

"Bessie will be disappointed."

"I need to leave."

"Office hours are over?" He raised his eyebrows.

She nodded.

"They'd page or call if they needed you."

"I still need to go." Now—or maybe never.

He looked deliberately at the second-story window of the log guesthouse and then back at her. "Chicken."

A sharp spate of laughter burst from her in spite of herself. "I came. I saw my patient and, I think, left her somewhat pleased." Okay, she had seen the ranch and had not self-destructed. And now she could go.

He looked at her thoughtfully for a moment. Oh, if he kept looking at her like that she was going to forget he was Henry's overbearing brother, that he literally held her future, her practice in the valley and her childhood home, in his hands.

"You can have a look around the place," he said into the silence.

"Really, I—" They seemed to have struck some sort of accidental truce. She didn't want to tax the accord by being too standoffish. On the other hand, a horrible feeling struck her. He had made an overture to her in the past. And if she fell for it a second time, shame on her. "I do need to go."

"Before you leave, I have something that might belong to one of your family members."

"Maybe some other time." But she couldn't get her stupid feet to move.

Go? Stay? Dither her brains out? Oh God. What happened to the woman in Chicago who had learned to go toe to toe with the biggest surgeon egos, the meanest patients, the scariest traumas?

"Henry left a note with it saying he thought it might be yours."

"Henry?"

"It'll only take a second."

"Okay. Show me what you've found."

He held out a hand toward the main house. Henry had probably found their stash of fool's gold. She and her sister had always hoped the shiny chunks they'd found were real gold, but Granddad always dashed their dreams.

Guy reached ahead, pulled open the door to the house and didn't goad her when she hesitated on the threshold before stepping inside.

"Whooo, whooo, chug, chug."

She laughed and Guy grumbled something behind her.

Her mother had written that Henry had loved the clock above the stove so much she'd insisted he keep it. It was so like Henry to do so, even though he'd had the rest of the house remodeled.

Ahead, the kitchen shined with new appliances, flooring and cupboards. To her right, the living room took her breath away. The ceiling had been vaulted, and the ceiling and walls were covered with a medium-stained pine to look as if they had been there for a few lifetimes instead of a couple of years.

"Very nice." The words seemed inadequate, but they were all she could find at the time.

From a little box on the fireplace mantel, Guy palmed a small object. When he walked over, he opened his hand. On his open palm lay a ring. A delicate gold band with a large solitaire ruby sparkled up at her.

She stared in disbelief. The ring looked as if it had been recently cleaned and polished, but she knew it was old, her grandmother's engagement ring, to be exact.

Maude hadn't seen the ring for well over two decades, since the day she had taken her mother's "most precious possession" from its secret hiding place, taken the family heirloom outside and lost it in the snow.

Maude's stomach began to roil.

Suddenly she knew if she didn't get out, she was going to hurl. Her hand flew to her mouth, and she ran.

GUY WATCHED THE little silver Subaru disappear around the bend leaving nothing behind but a curl of dust.

He held up the ring and watched the red stone glint in the sunlight. Then he closed his fist around it. He had expected her to snap it out of his hand. Her reaction didn't fit with the image of the woman he had carried all these years, the older woman trying to worm her way into his brother's heart and his fortune. Pieces of the puzzle he never had the time to examine too closely were looking more and more like an ill fit.

"You scare the good doctor away?"

"I might have." Guy nodded at Jake who ambled up to stand at his side.

The two of them watched the dust slowly disperse into the trees beside the road.

"She probably heard about your cooking."

"As a matter of fact, I offered to share the spread Bessie left this morning."

"Must be your personality, then."

Guy laughed and squeezed his hand tighter around the ring. "Must be. I'm hungry. Let's eat."

A little bell tinkled in the distance.

Jake started to move off, but Guy stopped him. "Let it go this time."

Jake turned back. "I'd've gladly done that team-building exercise this morning and you could have stayed here."

"Maybe I'll have to give you a raise."

"Wouldn't be big enough."

Guy chuckled and headed toward the house, Jake right behind him.

"I'll be there in a moment," Guy said. As they entered the house, he went to return the ring to its box on the mantel. He wondered what it was about the beautiful old thing that made Maude DeVane turn pale and flee. Then he remembered wanting to touch the rich brown curls that collected around her face.

Scaring her away might have done them both a favor.

"Food's on, boss," Jake called from the kitchen.

ON FRIDAY MORNING, Maude sat at the desk in her office and struggled to keep her eyes open. Irony. She thought of the hours during the last two nights when she had tried to make her tired eyes stay closed.

She would dream the image of Guy Daley smiling at her, reaching out and gently pushing her hair away from her face. His lips would cover hers, and she would kiss him back, until her eyes would snap open and in the darkness of the night she'd feel the loss as if it were real.

Then she'd go back to sleep and see the glint of red and gold disappear into the snow.

So much snow.

A light tap on her office door made her sit up straighter. "Yes, Arlene."

"Your first patient is ready for you." The office secretary had shown up like a trouper this morning, pencil behind her ear, ready for whatever came.

"Thanks." Maude had been surprised to see the office full of patients. Today there were even a few without appointments who "needed a minute with the doctor." She suspected most of them were there to see if Maudie had really turned into Dr. DeVane or if they should start looking elsewhere. Didn't matter. She'd see them. Show them they could have confidence in her.

Maybe she should have gotten some ice cream.

By the end of the day when the last patient left, she thought she might have gained a little ground. Taciturn bunch, most of them, so she could only hope.

She closed the last chart and put it in the "to file" stack on Arlene's desk. A nice soak in the tub was in order.

The phone on the desk rang. She looked at the decidedly anti-tub device and after the second ring picked it up. "This is Dr. DeVane."

"Dr. Avery. I need Dr. Avery right away, please."

"Dr. Avery is gone." Maude replied to the desperate-sounding voice on the other end of the line.

"But I need him. When will he be back?"

"Mrs. McCormack," Maude said when she recognized the nasal sound of the nearly hysterical woman.

"I need Dr. Avery."

"I'm afraid he's gone for good." The woman was the mother of a pair of little boys and the wife of a town council member. "What can I do to help you?"

"He can't be gone. He's not leaving until next week." The voice on the phone neared panic.

"Come to the clinic. I'm here now."

"No. I can't come to see you. Maybe I'll try his mobile phone. Maybe he'll—"

Suddenly, the line went dead.

Maude stared at the silent phone in her hand, then set it softly into the cradle. Should she try to call her, search for her? But where had the woman called from? Her car? Her home?

Reason told Maude to wait for another call. So she forwarded the clinic phone to her mobile and walked slowly to her car.

When Doc Avery was still in town and Maude was learning about his patients, Mrs. McCormack had found excuses not to have Maude see any of her family members.

Maude had tried to tell herself Mrs. McCormack was used to Dr. Avery. He had delivered her and her two children, after all. But when Mrs. McCormack had canceled her husband's appointment with Maude and had him wait an extra day to have his earache treated by Doc Avery, it seemed more than loyalty.

On the way home, Maude stopped at the grocery store, where she acquired dinner without even hesitating behind a display of anything. A few people smiled and some stared. When she was in her car and almost home, her phone rang.

"You've got to come. Come now. Sammy can hardly breathe. Please, help me."

"Where are you, Mrs. McCormack?" Sammy, the four-year-old McCormack. Red hair. They all had red hair.

"We— I was going to take him to Kalispell. I wanted him to see a doctor."

Maude let that one go.

"Where are you now?"

"Oh God, help me. I'm just outside of town."

"Can you get to the clinic in a few minutes? Safely?"

"Yes! Yes!"

"Put the phone down and drive, I'll be there before you get there." It didn't make sense to go out into the community to see the boy. She had none of her emergency equipment, and by the time the rescue crew could be mustered the boy would already be at the clinic.

Maude thumbed off the phone, parked and unsnapped the phone's cover. Tucked inside the casing, she kept the on call roster for the clinic staff. The roster let her know who expected to be called for emergencies. Abby was off, but Phyllis was a good nurse and her husband assured Maude that Phyllis would be there soon.

After she got to the clinic and prepared, she went outside to wait. A few minutes later, a car screamed up the street with the horn blowing. A van pulled over and let her by. The people of St. Adelbert did care for one another.

Mrs. McCormack's car nearly sideswiped another as she turned sharply onto the ramp. In one fluid motion, she screeched to a halt and jumped out of the car. The blue van pulled in behind her.

Maude wrenched open the rear car door and leaned in. The four-year-old looked up at her in distress. "It's all right, Sammy. We'll get you some help right away."

She lifted him from his safety seat, and with his body hot in her arms, she hurried into the clinic. His feathery red hair brushed her cheek. His little chest heaved in the struggle to move air in and out.

He pleaded for help with his eyes. "It'll be okay, Sammy. I'll make everything okay." At least his color was good.

Somewhere in a corner of her mind, she realized she had seen Guy Daley get out of the van. What did he want?

"What's wrong with him, Doctor?" Mrs. McCormack followed, breathless with fear.

"Tell me what's been happening, and I'll figure it out." She hurried into the room stocked with pediatric equipment, where she jerked the head section of the patient cart into the upright position with one hand, and then gently placed Sammy on the cart.

"Sammy, I'm going to put a mask on your face. Just like the jet pilots wear when they fly up in the big blue sky."

He nodded again and she slid a small mask onto his face to deliver moisturized oxygen. She looked up at Mrs. McCormack.

"He had a fever this morning, and then he started to cough like he couldn't stop. About two hours ago he started having a bit of trouble breathing and it kept getting worse. What are you going to do for him, Doctor?"

Maude smoothed back Sammy's hair. "I'm going to listen to your chest now, Sammy." She eased him forward and listened to the air squeak and wheeze as his small body tried to move air through tightened air passages. When she carefully rested his head again on the pillow, his skinny four-year-old arms lay freckled and limp beside him.

Maude took the ear thermometer and snapped his temperature—one hundred point eight; she could live with that—and then questioned the mother until she had all the information she needed to begin treatment.

"Sammy, I'm going to give you some medicine to help you breathe." She looked across the cart and spoke to Mrs. McCormack. "Stay right beside him."

"Don't leave us."

"I won't," Maude reassured her as she moved across the room to the emergency equipment. She set up the nebulizer to dispense medication in a mist and wheeled the apparatus over to the cart.

"Sammy, I'm going to have you breathe special air with special medicine in it." He gave her a heartrending look. "I want you to put your lips around this mouthpiece and breathe in as deeply as you can."

When she removed the oxygen mask and held the plastic mouthpiece of the hissing nebulizer near his lips, he pulled back. "No," and "Don't!" came out on two scratchy breaths. Maude could see in his eyes, he wanted to fend her off.

"Okay." She slid the oxygen back on his face and sat on the edge of the cart facing him. "Sammy, remember those jet pilots I mentioned before?"

He looked at her with wide eyes and gave her a tiny nod

as he struggled to bring the air into his lungs. She took hold of his hand and nodded to Mrs. McCormack to take his other.

"Now, close your eyes and open your mouth." He focused on his mother. She smiled a watery smile and nodded. He rested his head back and closed his eyes.

"Sammy, I want you to think about that big light blue sky where the pilots fly. Think about all that beautiful blue air." Maude lifted the mask slowly. "Now I'm going to lay this mouthpiece on your lips, and I want you to close your mouth on it just a little and only when you're ready. You're in control, just like the jet pilots."

As soon as she touched the plastic mouthpiece to his lips, his mouth closed. "Now take a breath through the special tube. Think of all that air out there in the big blue sky."

He breathed in the moist medicated air and coughed. His eyes flew open.

"Good. That's just what's supposed to happen." When he settled a bit she continued. "Now, take another breath from the tube and think about the nice blue air from the sky coming right down into the room and into your lungs."

He closed his mouth around the plastic piece again.

"Breathe deeply and let nice blue air fill your lungs."

He took a puff on the nebulizer and didn't cough.

"That's good, Sammy. You're getting the medicine. Take another breath."

Sammy breathed shallow breaths for a few minutes and then took what may have been the first good breath he had taken for hours and then another. His mother smiled and a tear slid down her cheek.

"Dr. DeVane, I'm here." Phyllis stepped to the foot of the cart. "Hello, Mrs. McCormack."

Maude looked around Phyllis to see Guy Daley standing in the hallway near the office.

Jake? Ms. Stone? Had something happened to one of the people from the ranch?

Maude placed a hand on Sammy's forehead. "Sammy, this is Phyllis. She's really good at getting the blue air into the room. She's going to stay with you and your mommy. Breathe from the machine until all the medicine is in your body.

"It should be just a few more minutes before the nebulizer is empty," she said to the robust, middle-aged nurse.

Phyllis covered Sammy's tiny hand with her large freckled one and took over holding the breathing apparatus.

"I'll be back when the medication is in, Mrs. McCormack," Maude said. "He's getting better already."

"Dr. Daley." She walked toward him. "Is there something wrong at the ranch?"

A child with a riot of dark red curls leaped out from behind him.

"Lexie!" Maude raised her hand for a high five and Lexie smacked it hard. She knew better than to try to hug the child.

"Maude, I didn't even know you were at the ranch the other day. You should have told me you were coming." Lexie jumped up and down to emphasize her words and then glared at her uncle Guy. "Nobody told me you were there at all until Bessie did."

Maude looked up at Guy and then back at Lexie. "Well, I didn't know you were coming out to Montana."

Lexie grinned at Maude with a mouth full of teeth still too big for her face. "That's probably my fault. I sort of didn't tell Uncle Guy I was coming."

"It's so good to see you. How long are you staying?"

Lexie looked up at Guy for a long, silent moment and shrugged one shoulder to her ear.

Maude hunkered down eye to eye with Lexie. "What brings you into town?"

"I didn't pack very well when I left home and I needed a few things."

"Does your uncle know what a good shopper you are?" Maude glanced over at Guy who held his expression neutral.

Lexie grinned. The freckles on her face seemed to dance. "I'm about to show him, but I wanted to say hi to you first."

"I'm glad you did."

"Promise you'll come out to see me at the ranch?"

Maude set aside the big dark thing in her distant past for the huge dark thing in this child's near past. "I won't let anything stop me." She wanted to shoot a warning scowl at Guy in case he thought to bring up the ring or if this truce business was some sort of game he had decided to run on her.

"Great. Can I go to Taylor's now?"

Guy nodded and Lexie took off for the drugstore down the street.

When Guy turned to looked at her, he smiled.

She liked it when he smiled.

"You were great with that little boy," he said.

"Thanks. He was so frightened. I'm glad I could help."

"But?"

"Nothing." She studied the sincere expression on his face. "I don't want to tell you."

"Who do you have left to tell?"

She looked over to the treatment room where she could see Sammy smiling at something Phyllis said. In Chicago and every other city she had been in, there were doctors everywhere to talk to. To complain, brag, discuss uncertainties. Here there was no one except him. "No one."

He stepped into the office and out of the view of the treatment room. "I'm a good listener."

When he said the words, he looked at her as if everything she had to say would be the most important words ever spoken. She wanted to believe that look. "His mother was ready to drive him to Kalispell because Dr. Avery is gone and all she had left was me."

"The boy's alive because she didn't."

She ducked her head. The thought of a child in jeopardy made her cringe. "If he had died in his mother's arms along the side of the highway, how do I not think that is my fault?"

"You aren't really that bad anymore, are you?"

She jerked her gaze up to his face. For one horrible moment, she didn't realize he was chiding her, and then she smiled. "I don't know if I'm beginning to like you, or if I should call Sheriff Potts and have you thrown out of town for harassing the new doctor."

She stepped around him and went back in to see Sammy.

"Dr. DeVane, I like the blue air. It's still in the room. See?" He took as deep a breath as he could. It still wasn't a normal breath, but he grinned and so did she.

"I'm glad you're feeling better, Sammy," she said to the boy. To Phyllis she said, "He can leave soon if he stays stable."

"Thank you." Sammy's mother gave her an apologetic smile.

"I'm glad you came, Mrs. McCormack. He has a virus. It should be gone completely in a few days." She paused and wrote a prescription and handed it to Mrs. McCormack. "If he starts having breathing problems again, use this medication. If it doesn't seem to be working, call me. You can call me anytime."

When Maude went back to the office to write up the notes on Sammy, Guy was still there, standing by the window. Outside, the clouds on the mountains were turning purple.

He turned as she stepped up beside him. "When you're finished, have dinner with Lexie and me. Then you can decide whether or not to call the sheriff."

"Why are you suddenly being nice to me?" Oops, that had sort of slipped unchecked out of her subconscious mind.

He looked at her for a long moment, his dark eyes probing. For a second she thought he might lean forward and kiss her, and she was not sure she would try to stop him.

"Dinner was Lexie's idea," he said at last. "And she lights up when she talks about you. There isn't a lot that does that in her life right now."

"You're making nice for the child?"

He nodded.

"Fair enough," she replied.

"I'll be back when she's finished shopping."

"I'm glad you brought the van."

He drew his dark eyebrows together, but she offered no explanation. She didn't have to; he'd find out soon enough.

She watched him walk away and realized she could do that all day. He walked like a movie star who knew the camera was still on, standing tall with strong strides taking chunks out of the world as if he owned it.

As a good distraction from her delusions, she started to write notes about her patient. This truce was too new to be believed, but as long as he didn't tell anyone in town he was a doctor, he wouldn't undermine her efforts to gain the town's trust. Once they got to know how well she could do the job, he could blab all he wanted because when he was gone, she'd still be there.

The outside door whooshed open.

"Where is he?" a loud voice demanded.

Phyllis stopped in her tracks just outside the office.

"It's Mr. McCormack, Phyllis. I'll talk to him." Maude said. "I'll talk to him."

Phyllis retreated to the treatment room, pulling the door closed after Mrs. McCormack scooted out.

"Hello, Mr. McCormack." Maude greeted the disheveled man striding through the hallway.

"I want to see him now and he better be okay." His voice filled the small clinic as he set a bead on his wife. Mrs. McCormack raced up to him with a wobbly smile.

He looked older than last week when he had been in to see Doc Avery. His red hair stuck out like windblown straw, and his nose was redder. He pushed his wife aside and charged toward Maude.

Maude stepped forward. "Mr. McCormack. I'm glad you came."

The friendly words made him pause and gave Maude time to get to the empty waiting room and away from the pediatric treatment room. He followed, as did Mrs. McCormack.

He spun unsteadily toward his wife. "Go back with the kid."

When she bowed her head and did as she was told, he whipped back around and drew himself up to try to tower over Maude.

Maude put her hands at her sides and relaxed her posture.

"Who told you to treat my son?" At least he wasn't yelling.

Just then, Guy and Lexie stepped into the doorway of the clinic in clear view of the waiting room, drawing her attention away.

"I'm talking to you." Mr. McCormack raised his voice again as he grabbed Maude's arm with a big freckled hand.

Guy started forward, but she gestured toward Lexie.

"That woman was supposed to take the kid to Kalispell."

*That woman?* His words didn't slur, but she could smell the alcohol. Maude put her hand gently on top of his and left it there. When she glanced at the entrance, Guy and Lexie were gone. "You're upset, Mr. McCormack."

"Damn right I'm upset. I told her not to bring him to a woman doctor."

Maude squeezed gently on the hand that was becoming a vise grip on her arm. "There are good facilities in Kalispell."

"I don't want a woman treating my kid, especially one who can't get a job anyplace else."

Maude hadn't seen that one coming. The rumor mill was more vicious than she had imagined. She squeezed his hand the way a mother might a troubled child. "I can see how you'd want Sammy to have the best care there is."

"The best care." He pulled her toward him until they were toe to toe. The smell of alcohol washed over her, but she refused to bristle. He was itching for a fight and he wasn't going to find one here. "The best care. That's why we're still looking for a replacement for Doc Avery. A real doctor."

They had a "real" doctor. Maude buried the confusion his words caused.

"Your son's a brave boy, Mr. McCormack, and he's doing fine."

He stepped back and threw her arm away. "He's—so little." Tears filled the man's eyes where before there had been intoxicated rage.

At that moment Sammy came running out and grabbed his dad's leg. "Hot dogs. Daddy, I want hot dogs."

Maude spoke up. "You and his mother can take him home now." She didn't want to send the boy away with such a man. She wanted all children to live happy lives like her friend Sally's kids. *He's trying to get help,* Dr. Avery had told her.

McCormack leaned down and scooped up his son. Hugging the boy tightly, he ran out the door with Mrs. McCormack following. Thank God, the alcohol had not destroyed his humanity and his love for his son.

Maude hugged her arms around her chest. "Still looking for a replacement for Doc Avery," she murmured. Could that be true? Or was it the intoxicated notion of a distraught father?

"Maude, are you all right?"

She looked up to see Guy standing alone in the doorway.

# CHAPTER FOUR

MAUDE WASN'T SURE how to react to the concern in Guy's voice, so she put on an automatic smile and stepped past him into the hallway. "I'm fine, thank you."

"You took quite a chance with that man." He scowled at her.

Anger and disapproval from this man, she understood. "So, we're back to that, are we?"

He crossed his arms over his chest, but his look softened. "The man was dangerous."

"He's never lifted a hand to anyone, not even his wife."

"He could have easily crossed that line today."

"I have to see them as they come to me. They have no one else in the valley to go to."

Lexie appeared in the doorway burdened with bags.

"I'm starving." She gave an exaggerated sigh and shoved the bags at Guy.

He raised his eyebrows and Lexie giggled. "Well, you locked the van. We're not in Chicago, you know."

"Did you buy out the drugstore?" he said as he hefted the bags by their plastic handles.

"I could show you the stuff in the bags, Uncle Guy, but there's things in there that it would be icky for you to see."

A steady look passed between man and child.

"I'll get my jacket and say goodbye to Phyllis," Maude said as uncle and niece headed out the door with the bags divided between them.

Guy and Lexie were stowing Lexie's purchases in the van when Maude came outside.

"Where should we eat?" Guy asked when they were finished.

"Alice's," Lexie volunteered quickly.

Since she was hungry enough to eat anything, Maude agreed. And as they headed across the street to the diner, sprinkles of cold rain began to fall.

Lexie sprinted ahead and held the door open for them.

Several heads twisted on their stalks as the three of them entered the premier business in St. Adelbert, if longevity were the measure.

"You two sit over there." Lexie pointed to the booth seat opposite the one she dropped into. "I'm tired and I need to stretch out." With that, she put her feet up and grinned at them.

Maude cast a glance at Guy and the two of them sat down opposite to the so-obviously-plotting little girl. Maude did her best not to let any part of her body touch the man next to her. Lexie was going to lose this one.

As soon as they were settled, Lexie leaped from her seat. "I'll be right back."

"Wait until we order."

"Can't." She dashed off in the direction of the restrooms.

"I have so much control over her." Guy gave Maude a wry smile.

"She's a good kid. What was that look you gave each other back in the clinic?"

"I told her she couldn't buy makeup."

"Oh, tough one."

"She had mascara smeared almost down to her chin when she got to the ranch. I suspect makeup was how she conned so many people into thinking she was older. I have all summer until she has any real complaint. Who's she going to wear it for, the horses?"

"Horses? Wait. She came across country alone?"

"We've already had the 'it's dangerous' discussion, but I doubt that would stop her from trying it again."

Maude couldn't help but think how much he reminded her of Henry when he spoke about Lexie. When he smiled, it lifted his features, and as his laughter rumbled through her, she felt things she never felt for Henry.

"So, the rumor's true."

"Jake!" Maude nearly jumped from the vinyl booth and then turned to gape at the cowboy, until she realized he was only conjecturing what the tongues would be saying tomorrow about the woman doctor and that guy from the Whispering Winds Ranch.

"Hello, Jake. Have a seat." Guy pointed to the empty booth across from them.

"Dr. DeVane, boss. No, thanks. Not staying."

"Jake says he'll take me home." Lexie appeared behind the cowboy.

Guy looked between Lexie and Jake and then back at Jake. "What brings you to town?"

"Ms. Stone wanted a few things." Jake held up a couple of bags from the drugstore.

"I never thought of you as an errand boy," Guy said.

"I never did, either, until being an errand boy seemed like a small slice of heaven compared to—" Jake stopped and grinned.

Lexie snorted. Not much got by her. "Jake, let's go. These two are, um—"

"Boring?" Guy finished for her.

"Yeah, that's the word."

"I think we should wait until your uncle gives you permission."

"I thought you wanted to spend some time with Maude." Guy gave Lexie one of his officious, steady looks.

"Maude says she'll come and see me at the ranch. Come on, Jake. Let's go before he thinks of a reason for me not to go."

"I thought you were hungry." Maude took a stab at keeping the girl there. She wasn't sure she wanted to be left alone with a man so recently her enemy.

"I'm more tired now." She stretched and yawned, both fake. "Besides, Bessie will have something for me."

After Jake left in Lexie's tow, Maude moved to the opposite side of the table and they gave their orders to the waitress.

Guy settled in the middle of the booth across from Maude. "Jake says she plays me easier than a one-holed fife."

"He told Henry the same thing."

"Henry couldn't do enough for her, trying to make up for not knowing she existed, I guess."

"It wasn't his fault. They were little more than children when Lexie was born. Henry was never sure whether it was Lexie's mother or her mother's parents that wanted Lexie kept secret for so long." Maude didn't know why she felt she needed to defend Henry to his brother.

"You and Henry spent a lot of time together. I don't think I appreciated your friendship as I should have."

"Is that a request for friendlier terms between us?" Maude asked.

"Feelers. I'm not sure I gave you a real chance in Chicago."

She looked at him for a long moment, wondering how he could think he gave her any chance at all.

He held up a hand. "All right, I shut you out."

She nodded. "You were busy being the best, and Henry never thought he fit into that picture."

"Thank you," they each said after the waitress dropped off their food and beverages.

"I guess I invited a blunt opinion." The expression on his face gave away nothing of what he was feeling.

She smiled and then lobbed another volley. "You scared the hell out of me on my first day of emergency room rotation." He frowned and she continued. "After the resident told me who you were, I was in kind of a state of awe to meet the great Dr. Daley in person. I remember wondering how many years of practice it would take me to be able to intimidate everyone in the room with one look."

He opened his mouth and closed it. This was the first time she noticed he had a small scar at the corner of his right eyebrow. She wondered how he got it.

"Did I go too far?" Maude asked.

A glimmer of amusement touched his dark eyes. "I remember the shock on your face when I said to pack Henry up, I was taking him to a different hospital."

"It's been several years, but I think you said something like, 'to a different hospital where they had doctors who knew what they were doing.'"

"When Henry told me he went to see you, I was sure he was going to tell me you quit."

She laughed a little. "Maybe you were the reason I stayed put and finished."

He took a drink of his milk and when he put it down, he rested his hand on the table, his fingertips a scant inch from hers. She noted the strong hand against the checkered tablecloth. Her fingers tingled in anticipation of what it would be like if he stroked them. And then if he stroked higher…

"Henry thought a lot of you." His words broke the dizzying spell.

"I thought a lot of him." And Guy had kissed her to prove she wasn't good enough for Henry, at least that's what it seemed like at the time.

Maude's phone vibrated. "Excuse me," she said as she wrestled it out of her jacket pocket.

*Sheriff Potts.*

She looked at Guy. "I have to take this."

GUY WATCHED Dr. Maude DeVane push open the inside door of the restaurant leading to the small glass foyer that protected the patrons from the bitter winter elements. Right now, it sheltered her from the rain falling out in the dark street.

*Little more than children,* she had said of Henry and the girl who had been Lexie's mother. It was true at the time, and Guy wasn't sure he ever thought of Henry as anything but a child, and now that was all that would ever be between him and his brother.

Maude DeVane was the last person he expected to be discussing his brother with. Yet she had been the one who spent more time with Henry than he when they all lived in Chicago.

Maybe it was time he got to know Dr. DeVane better. For Lexie's sake.

And maybe for his own. The urge to touch her hand as it lay on the table only an inch from his, to apologize— No, apologizing had not been his topmost thought. He wanted to touch her. Feel the softness of her skin. To give in to the feelings he had had for her since a dark and rainy night so many years ago.

OUT IN THE SMALL FOYER, Maude pressed her phone to her ear to shut out the pounding of the rain. "Go on, Sheriff."

"Dr. DeVane, I don't know if it's the two chocolate brownies I had after dinner—well, okay, three, but I'm having some indigestion that won't go away. I've had it for about an hour now."

The sheriff, who took his responsibility to the small valley very seriously, sounded worried, and the big lawman didn't worry easily.

"Sheriff," Maude said, using a calm it took years of practice to master. "Have you ever had this before?" A stomach problem, or a problem with his heart? She had to differentiate, or a man could die.

"Well, I might've had it last week when I was chasing the DuMont boys."

"How do you feel otherwise?"

"I got a little of that bursitis back in my left shoulder, but other than that I'm fine." He gave a small chuckle she knew to be forced.

"Where are you?"

"Home."

"I'd better take a look at you." Tonight would be a great night for St. Adelbert to have a rescue squad that wasn't comprised of volunteers. "Come into the clinic now."

"My wife's out playing cards with the girls. It'll scare

her if she hears I've gone to the clinic. Don't know why I called. Nervous, I guess. I'll stop by in the morning."

Fear from the big man left Maude feeling cold. She pulled her jacket closed around her.

"Do you have someone to drive you?"

"Yes'm. One of the deputies stopped by."

"Come in now. I'll check you out."

"Yes, ma'am."

"Lights and sirens, Sheriff Potts."

"Yes, ma'am." The sheriff should be scared. It probably wasn't the brownies causing heartburn. It was probably decades of brownies causing a heart attack.

"Sheriff, take an aspirin, if you have one on hand, chew it carefully and swallow it."

"Yes, ma'am."

She pocketed her phone as Guy opened the door to the foyer.

"Sorry, I have to go." She turned, pushed open the outside door and started out into the rain.

Guy's grip on her arm stopped her and pulled her back under the rain-battered awning. "What's happening?"

"I've got a patient coming in."

He pulled her closer and held her by both arms. Reflexively, she raised her hands and then balled them into fists instead of putting them on his chest as she wanted to do. She tried to concentrate on a raindrop trickling down her face, but all she could see was the darkness of his eyes and hear was the pounding of her heart and feel was the need to kiss him.

Slowly, as if time had no meaning, he lowered his mouth to hers and the fire burst inside her. Flames raged through her senses and threatened to consume everything except her desire for him—until the doctor took over. She pushed back, dipped in for one more quick kiss, and then said, "I've got to go."

He let go and she dashed out into the rain and across the street to the clinic. Inside she leaned against the wall for several seconds to get her composure, then flipped on the lights.

Everything had to be business now. She called Phyllis back in and a tech for backup. Even though the nurse always inventoried and restocked before closing the clinic down, Maude checked the resuscitation equipment. After that, she pulled the sheriff's old medical records. All of his past tests, including his electrocardiogram and other heart studies, had been normal. His only complaint in the past had been indigestion for which Dr. Avery had prescribed an acid blocker.

Finished and ready, she paced, holding on to a sliver of hope that the sheriff was right about the symptoms being related to the chocolate brownies.

"Get here in time for me to help you, Sheriff," she said quietly into the pounding of the rain outside the door.

Sheriff Potts had been a deputy when Maude left town. He had grown into the man the whole valley depended on for safety, to settle arguments and for he and his wife to oversee the annual St. Adelbert-valley picnic.

The squad's siren in the distance heightened her senses, and as red and blue lights began to bounce off the cream-colored walls, she pushed the patient cart outside. Rain hammered the overhang and cold air hit her face, but she noted them as of interest only. Her patient was her focus now.

The deputy jumped out of the squad. "He doesn't look so good, Dr. DeVane."

"We'll get him on the cart."

"He'll yell at us." The young deputy's voice nearly squeaked with anxiety.

"Yeah, but we can take it."

He flashed a nervous grin at her as she pushed the cart closer to the squad car.

Sheriff Potts swung his feet out the door of the car and when he saw the cart, bowed his head. "I just need antacid."

"Come on, Sheriff, pretend you're one of the volunteer wounded during a disaster drill and hop on." The deputy held out a hand to the sheriff.

"Dr. DeVane, thanks for coming." The big man pushed up out of the car and climbed onto the gurney without help.

"Glad I could be here for you, Sheriff." She gave him a reassuring pat on the shoulder. The ashen-gray color of his skin made her grateful he hadn't driven to Kalispell to get help. "I'm going to put some oxygen on you and we'll get you inside."

She slid the prongs of the translucent green tubing into his nose, and he put his head on the pillow without further protest.

"Good evening, Dr. DeVane." Phyllis trundled up to the cart and took hold of the foot while Maude steered from the head.

After they entered the building, Sheriff Potts grabbed the deputy's arm. "Go get my wife and bring her here. She's playing cards at Sharon's house."

"Right away, Sheriff." The deputy seemed relieved to have something meaningful to do and darted away.

"What's wrong with me?" the sheriff asked as they wheeled him into the largest of the four treatment rooms, the trauma room set up for the most serious cases.

"We'll have some answers shortly. In the meantime, I'm going to slip an intravenous line into your arm."

By the time Maude was finished with the IV, Phyllis had connected him to the cardiac monitor and there was no doubt.

"You're having a heart attack, Sheriff. A blocked blood vessel is cutting off the blood flow to your heart muscle. I need your permission to administer a drug to help break up the clot. If we can get the blood flowing to the muscle we might be able to minimize the damage, maybe even prevent damage altogether."

The sheriff closed his eyes for a moment.

Phyllis slipped the monitoring device on his finger to check his blood oxygen level—it looked good—and then slipped a cuff on his arm to measure his blood pressure.

"Do what you gotta do, Doctor. My daughter's getting married next month and I need to give her away." He let go of denial and went right for practical reality. She would expect nothing less from Sheriff Potts.

"Phyllis will prepare the medication now. I need to explain a few things and have you sign a consent."

He nodded.

"While the medication is going in, Sheriff, I'll get the transport helicopter on its way. We need to get you to Kalispell where they can study your heart and find out exactly what's going on."

"Won't the medicine fix it?"

"It might, temporarily."

He frowned and looked up at her. "I know she can't go in the evac helicopter, but I don't want Flora driving to Kalispell tonight."

"You know the people of St. Adelbert will line up to volunteer to drive her there," Maude reminded him.

Again he nodded. "They're a good bunch."

Phyllis hung a small intravenous bag and piggybacked the needle into the intravenous line already in place. She reached up to start the medication when the cadence of the cardiac monitor changed from steady to irregular and, almost as suddenly, to a rapid rate.

"V-tach," Phyllis said quietly when the sheriff's heartbeat turned dangerous.

"What is that, Doctor? I feel…" The sheriff's voice trailed off and the heart monitor's alarm squawked.

"Sheriff, Sheriff." Maude tightened her grip on the sheriff's shoulder and shook him. When he didn't respond, she lowered the head of the cart to flat.

Phyllis silenced the alarm.

Maude palpated his neck for signs that his abnormally beating heart was still pumping blood. "Pulse is faint." So faint she hoped it wasn't a wish on her part.

"He's still breathing," Phyllis said.

"He's big and he's out. We'll cardiovert." Maude instructed Phyllis to charge the machine that would hopefully shock the sheriff's heart rhythm back to normal, or at least to a rhythm that would get enough oxygen to his brain.

"You hang in there, Sheriff," Phyllis said to the unconscious man as she efficiently slapped conduction gel pads for the procedure in place and positioned the paddles on top.

"Clear." Phyllis paused and then pressed the trigger. The machine almost immediately directed a jolt of electricity through the sheriff's chest wall toward his heart.

"Still V-tach." Maude kept the calm in her voice. Into the intravenous line, she pushed a drug designed to help stabilize the sheriff's heart rhythm.

The sound of the clinic's outside doors opening reverberated through the room. A child's shrill scream quickly followed.

"Help us. Somebody please help us," a woman pleaded.

Maude looked up. "Go. I've got this." She took the paddles from Phyllis, checked the machine to see that it had been charged to a higher level.

"Clear," Maude said quietly as part of the protocol to make sure no one got the dangerous electric current except the patient in need, and then she pressed the discharge buttons. The sheriff's heart rhythm remained stubbornly unchanged and potentially deadly.

"*Oomph.*" Phyllis nearly plowed into Guy Daley as he stepped into the room. She quickly darted around him and disappeared.

"Dr. Daley," Maude said as calmly as she could while she recharged to give the sheriff's obstinate heart an even higher dose of electrical shock.

"I can help," he said and frowned at the sight of the unconscious sheriff.

"Clear." Maude discharged the paddles again to no avail. "We can handle this."

The child wailed down the hallway.

She started the machine recharging to the highest possible setting.

"It's a three-year-old with a head laceration. Lot of blood, but doesn't look serious," Guy offered.

"It's kind of you. Make the boy comfortable if you can. Bert, a tech, should be here soon and he can take over until I get there," Maude said, keeping her attention focused on her patient. "And please send Phyllis back in."

Guy disappeared from the room.

If this shock didn't work…

"He's not breathing anymore," Maude said quietly to Phyllis, as the nurse stepped back into the room.

Phyllis grabbed an airway and slid it deftly in the sheriff's mouth to move his tongue out of the way of his air passage. Still no air passed.

"Pulse is gone," Maude said and indicated to Phyllis to begin artificial respirations with the bag and mask apparatus.

The ready light illuminated on the defibrillator.

"Clear," she commanded.

Phyllis stepped away, ready to resume breathing for the sheriff as soon as the jolt of electricity had been delivered.

Maude discharged the full capacity of the machine into the dying sheriff's body, and—

—his heart stopped beating altogether. Phyllis replaced the breathing mask and squeezed the attached bag to force well-oxygenated air into the sheriff's lungs.

Maude waited as one second went into two. A voice inside her head screamed *do something*. I am, her calmer side responded, I'm having faith in the miracle of the human heart.

Maude held her breath in the abyss of the heart monitor's silence. After the third second of quiet, one single heartbeat blipped on the monitor—and then another. Within about five seconds of total time, an interval that had seemed like all eternity, a regular succession of beats filed across the screen.

Sheriff Potts inhaled on his own.

GUY APPROACHED the screaming child. Echoes of the past he had left behind rippled through him. The nearly frantic young woman tried her best to hold a gauze over the boy's wound.

"Hi. I'm Dr. Daley. Dr. DeVane has asked me to take a look at this little guy."

The woman seemed instantly relieved, and as he expected, the boy didn't stop screaming long enough to acknowledge his presence. Guy smiled. Normal kid behavior. He liked to see that. It helped to rule out brain injury.

"What's his name?"

"Charlie." The woman sounded hopeful.

"Charlie, I'm going to fix your head. Mom?" He raised his eyebrows at the woman.

"Mommy. I want Mommy," the boy cried.

"Aunt Sarah." Her voice trembled. "We were playing and he fell against the coffee table."

"Did he lose consciousness?"

She looked at him with alarm. "I don't think so. He's been like this since the moment he hit his head. I—I promised to take care of him."

"And you are. He's a kid. He bumped his head, and we'll take care of him." He hunkered down to speak to the child at little-boy level. "Charlie, Aunt Sarah is going to bring you to a room down the hall and we'll get you patched up like new."

The child screamed louder.

When they got to the room, Guy indicated Aunt Sarah should put Charlie on the cart. "If you'd like to wait in the waiting room, Charlie and I are going to have a chat."

Aunt Sarah glanced skeptically from the screaming child to Guy.

"He'll be fine." He gave her his best doctor–benevolent God smile.

She smiled back at him and fled.

Guy turned to the little boy. "Charlie," he asked calmly, "do you have a doggy?"

MAUDE HEARD THE child go abruptly silent and prayed that was a good thing.

"Sheriff, can you hear me? Sheriff." She shook the sheriff by the shoulder.

The man on the cart remained still, his chest rising and falling, the monitor cascading the beats of his heart. Maude and Phyllis looked at each other over the cart.

Without warning, Sheriff Potts bucked and tried to cough. Then he reached up and pushed the mask off his face. Maude took the plastic airway from his mouth.

"I went out for a bit, didn't I, Doctor?" he asked.

"Your heart wasn't beating normally and you weren't getting enough oxygen to your brain to keep you conscious. Sort of a protective reflex the body does under the circumstances. Glad you're back." Very, very glad. "We've given you medication to stabilize your heart's rhythm. I think you'll stay with us now."

Phyllis slid an oxygen mask on his face. "Relax and breathe, Sheriff."

"Walfred," Mrs. Potts called from the doorway. Flora Potts had a sweet face and was small in stature even if you didn't compare her to her massive husband.

"Sorry, honey." The sheriff held out a big hand to her. "I didn't mean to mess things up."

"You big lug." She grabbed his hand with both of hers. "You didn't mess up anything." The chiding in her voice spoke of old love.

Maude smiled. Perhaps, she'd have old love someday.

"What happened, Dr. DeVane?" Mrs. Potts asked.

With the sheriff's permission, Maude explained what had occurred and then told both of them what the near future would hold.

"Can I stay with him until he leaves, Doctor?" Flora put her head on her husband's shoulder.

"Please do, Mrs. Potts," Maude said to the sheriff's wife and then turned to Phyllis. "I'm going to call evac and see the other patient."

Arranging for transport always took longer than she thought it should, but soon she had all the details of the flight to Kalispell ironed out.

Now to see what the tech, who should be here by now, was up to with the child. The screaming hadn't restarted, and again Maude didn't know if that was good or bad. She hurried down the hall.

As she approached the treatment room, the soft murmur of Guy's voice almost mesmerized her. What was Guy Daley still doing in with the patient? Where was Bert?

The scene she beheld when she entered the room fed her worst fear. The child lay inert on the table, unconscious.

Dr. Daley sat contentedly sewing up the wound on the child's forehead with fine blue thread.

"Oh my God! What are you doing? Is he—"

"Sleeping? Yes." He looked up at her briefly and then returned to what he was doing. "But not for long if the house doctor keeps making so much noise."

She lowered her voice. "How do you know he's asleep? Maybe he's—"

"He's not. I'll be finished in a second and I'll wake him."

"But what—"

"He's fine."

"You could at least let me finish a sentence."

"His name is Charlie and his doggy's name is Bella."

"Arabella the Gatekeeper to be exact, a terror of a Scottish terrier. This is Charlie Thompson, and I can't believe you got him to sleep. Crying and screaming are his standard ways of communicating even on a good day."

Guy shrugged and smiled. "He likes to talk about Bella." The child stirred.

Maude wanted to put on sterile gloves and yank the suture equipment from him. He was practicing medicine in her clinic on one of her patients without her permission. She didn't even know if he still had a medical license.

But Charlie came first. If he awoke now, there would just be more trauma in his little life.

The row of tiny stitches pulled the wound together without puckers or lumps; it looked as good as anything she could have done. The "everything in its place" Thompsons would approve. Unless they found out their child was being treated by a man who wasn't a doctor anymore.

"Not bad for a seminar leader, but you and I have things to talk about."

He nodded and placed another stitch.

"I'm going to go check on Sheriff Potts." And please be practicing medicine legally in Montana, she thought.

"Charlie. Hey, big guy," she heard Guy say tenderly to the little boy as she strode out of the room.

"Bella got a blue collar for her birthday party," Charlie's small voice responded.

Once the sheriff was safely turned over to the medical transport team, Maude sought out Charlie's Aunt Sarah.

Sarah jumped up and Charlie stayed contentedly on the couch with red Saf-T-Pop juice running down his chin. "Thank you, Dr. DeVane. Dr. Daley said you'd need some information from us."

"Excuse me, Dr. DeVane," Bert said as he ambled up to her. "Sorry it took so long for me to get here."

The tech wore a questioning expression on his usually kind face. Phyllis must have told him Guy Daley was Dr. Daley. It ought to take the whole valley about twenty-five seconds to know she was not the only doctor around.

Maude could hear them now. *Oh, goody. A real doctor, a male doctor.* How long, she wondered, before they came in a mob and ran her out of town so the man doctor could take over?

Now she should go face the other doctor. Find out if it was even legal for him to practice in Montana. First, she was going to go into her office and pull all her hair out. There. That would give them something to talk about.

# CHAPTER FIVE

GUY STOOD OUTSIDE the clinic's entrance, under the ramp's overhang. He considered leaving, but he'd overstepped boundaries tonight in more than one way. He'd stay and face whatever Dr. DeVane's response would be.

When Charlie Thompson's plaintive wail had burst through the background of the constant patter of rain a few minutes ago, he knew she was checking out his unasked-for handiwork. Stirring things up, making the boy cry, and in her position he'd have done the same thing. Examined his patient thoroughly.

He wondered how mad she was. Hopping, seeing red, stark raving; all of the above, probably.

He tugged his collar up against the cool wind bringing a spattering of rain under the canopy.

She wouldn't be angry about the job he'd done. He was licensed to practice medicine in the state of Montana, but she didn't know that. He didn't have specific privileges to treat patients at St. Adelbert's clinic and no permission to treat another doctor's private patient. Yup. She'd be mad.

Hell, he hadn't meant to sew up the kid's head. He'd meant to get things ready for her, lend a benign hand in a tough situation, but as soon as he opened the suture kit for her to use, it had just seemed natural.

Who was he kidding? He had sewn the kid's head up because what he really wanted to do was to dump the child with Dr. DeVane and take over the resuscitation. The thought surprised him, but it probably shouldn't. He'd spent over ten years making life-and-death decisions, and then the day came when he thought he'd never be able to do it again.

"Dr. Daley?"

Guy turned to see the nurse, Phyllis, standing behind him. He hadn't realized it, but the child no longer cried. Even the rain had stopped falling.

"Dr. DeVane said to tell you she'll come out to the ranch and talk to you tomorrow."

*Go away, but you're not off the hook, buddy.* Guy wasn't surprised at being sent away. He liked to be alone after he'd done serious life saving. Playing a godlike figure used to both elate and humble him. Now he knew the great doctor thing was all a myth. "Thanks, Phyllis."

MAUDE PLUCKED a piece of light brown toast from the toaster and spread on a wickedly large amount of huckleberry jam. She had purchased it at the diner in town. Some of the "Alices" would have challenged the bears in the wild to pick these berries, and their daring and adventurous spirits added to the deliciousness of the jam. Made it special enough for a celebration. And she had something to celebrate.

The doctor in Kalispell had called to say her rapid response time and her treatment had saved the sheriff's life. And, as icing, she got to him in time to save his heart muscle and preserve normal heart function.

The sheriff would be fine and, with a few lifestyle changes, would be for a long time.

Outside her kitchen window, dew glistened on the leaves of the small mountain birch in her backyard. She had hoped to coax the tree into a healthy growth spurt; now she just wanted the chance to try.

Most people would know now about the other doctor in the valley. It wasn't a small leap to think McCormack and the rest of his cronies on the town council would be all over Dr. Daley as soon as possible.

Well, she thought as she celebrated another bite of her toast and jam, she was just going to have to prove she was as good a choice as any doctor they could have found.

She'd saved the sheriff, and that had to count for something.

Her pocket hummed. Maude resisted taking another bite of toast and plucked the buzzing phone from her robe pocket. The caller ID said, *Mom.*

She thumbed on the speaker and put the handset on the table. "Hi, Mom!" She took a bite of toast, because the first thing her mother would do was complain about the caller ID.

"Oh, dear. I'll never get used to that caller ID thing." Her mother's voice blasted into the breakfast nook. "It's so unnerving to have you do that."

Maude swallowed and reduced the phone's volume. "How are you, and how's the old grouch?"

"I miss you, dear, and your father is fine, but thinking of you living so far away and not even on our ranch, it just about kills him." Her mother's voice faltered.

Maude knew "just about kills him" meant her father would distractedly agree when her mother suggested Maude should move to Great Falls.

"It's okay, Mom. I miss the ranch, too." She would

usually tell this lie. It mollified her mother. But today she had something different to add. "I'm going out there as soon as I finish at the office."

"You are? Oh, I'm so happy! Then you can finally say goodbye properly and move to the city with us." Her mother's enthusiasm almost bubbled from the handset.

"Mom."

"I know, dear, but I thought after you saw how happy your father and I are here in Great Falls, you'd want to come here and live with us. The ranch is gone. If you could just let it go, you would come to your senses about moving to town."

"I *am* glad you're happy and I'll come for a visit soon."

"Don't come for a visit, move to town."

"St. Adelbert is a town."

"Don't be silly, dear. It's a tiny dot on the map and besides there aren't even any—"

"Suitable men? As it turns out, I'm still not looking for one." The image of Guy Daley's dark, searching eyes popped into her head, and she squeezed her own shut to get rid of it, only to remember the feeling of his lips on hers.

Her eyes snapped open, and she tried to concentrate on what her mother was saying.

"…and when you are, will you please move here where the market is bigger?"

"I might visit for a little while, nab a likely candidate, and head here to the back country where I can keep him captive so he'll never get away."

Her mother's laughter was tinged with nervousness as if she believed Maude might actually be planning such things. "Maybe you wouldn't have to work that hard to keep a man—if you could ever find one."

"Mother."

"And we really do miss having you here."

"Mom, there are people here who—"

"—who need you. I know. Let Dr. Avery find someone else to help him."

"Dr. Avery's gone."

There was a long pause. "You're by yourself?"

*Don't start, Mom.*

She could still hear her mother's words from over the years. *You'll never make it into college. No medical school will take you. That residency is too hard for you.* The litany had started with, *you're not as pretty as Amanda—or as smart, dear.* And would end with a spoken or implied, *Amanda could have—fill in the blank.* Maude had always been the also-ran, the supporting actor, the ardent fan, but never the player—in the eyes of her parents—in the eyes of the community of St. Adelbert.

But she knew she could change that.

"Mom, I'm fine."

"Well, if you moved here, you'd at least have your family as backup."

*Mama, I have something I have to tell you about that night.*

*No, Maudie. I don't want you to talk about that ever again.*

Backup was not her mother's strong suit.

"How's Amanda, Mom?"

"She's the same." Her mother's tone held the usual brittleness when they talked about Amanda. Maude knew that was all she'd get on the subject of her sister.

"Did you call for anything in particular, Mom?"

"We'd like to come for a visit. Do you think you could find any time for us?"

"Well, let me think. I've got to build a cage for the man I'm going to catch…"

"Very funny, dear. I'm being serious."

"Of course, I'll have time for you. There aren't that many sick people." And half of them didn't come to see her anyway.

"I thought we'd come tomorrow for the ice-cream social and be there for the All Valley Picnic next weekend. We thought it would be a good time to catch up with our friends."

"Oh, the ice-cream social was to be a goodbye party for Dr. Avery, but he's gone, so I can't imagine why they would still hold it. Come to St. Adelbert anyway. It would be good to see you."

"Is the Swanson's motel still clean and well kept?"

"My guest room always awaits the two of you."

"That's so kind of you, dear. I have to go now. Oh, and I'll have a trunk full of samples for you to look at. Bye-bye."

Her mother hung up before Maude could protest. Samples. Her mother had been so determined to decorate Maude's house, Maude had decided to let her. It made her mother happy, and it had sounded so easy at the time.

BY THE TIME MAUDE had finished Saturday office hours, the sun had sunk almost down to the mountaintops. She had spent the day seeing people who were there to check her out. Most of them had no medical need at all. To their credit, not one of them mentioned Doc Avery or Dr. Daley.

When she got to her car, the youngest of Sheriff Potts's deputies was there waiting, looking as if he had news. Maude hoped it was nothing dire.

He tipped his hat. "Dr. DeVane, I just wanted to let you

know Ida Hawes passed sometime in the middle of the night. Mr. Hawes called us up this morning."

"Poor Mr. Hawes. The office called the coroner, I assume."

"Yes, ma'am. He seemed—Mr. Hawes seemed—uh. Well, I'm worried about him when his family leaves in a couple days."

Maude thought of the elderly man who had been seeing his wife through mental decline for the past several years. "I'll be sure to visit him in a day or two, find out if he needs anything."

"Thank you, Doctor. I was hoping you'd say that." Then a great big grin crossed his face. "Mrs. Potts called the office today. They're going to let the sheriff out on Monday, but she's going to keep him in Kalispell for a few days."

A wise decision on Mrs. Potts's part, Maude thought. Keep her husband away from his job and keep him in a place where he might get a bit of relaxation. "Thank you, Deputy."

He bid her farewell and marched off to the squad car.

FOREST AND MOUNTAIN meadows flitted by Maude's window as she drove to the ranch. She knew she'd never tire of the beautiful drive through this wild country. But she was a little alarmed that when she arrived at the ranch, the feeling of coming home was stronger than it had been yesterday.

And there was the ring. She had tried not to think about the ring since Guy had tried to give it to her. She didn't want it. If he brought it up, she'd tell him just that. The beautiful ruby was supposed to be a sign of love, not of a destroyed life.

"Hello, Dr. DeVane." Bessie, the housekeeper, greeted her at the ranch house door with a dish towel in her hand. *Always working at something,* Henry had said about the cook and housekeeper. "It's good to see you again."

Maude had met Bessie when Henry brought her to Chicago last year…*to see the tall buildings and all that flat land,* Bessie had said.

"Hi, Bessie. It's good to see you again, too." Henry's death lay between them, a heavy weight neither of them brought up. "Is Dr. Daley in?"

"He took the executives out to the rock climbing wall today and I haven't seen him since."

"Did all the executives go out on the wall?"

Bessie's face suddenly lit up. "Yeah, can you imagine she'd go?"

Relieved, Maude smiled back. "I'm glad Ms. Stone is feeling better."

"Must have been something you said to her."

Maude wasn't so sure it was anything she had done. "Is Lexie here?"

Bessie wiped a bit of something from the woodwork of the living-room doorway as they walked through. "She's been up in her room all day. Mad at her uncle, I think. The door on the right at the end of the hall, if you want to go up."

"Thanks, Bessie. I will."

Maude admired the photos and paintings that decorated the pine walls of the stairs and the hallway. Some were modern, some old, and all of the Wild West. Henry had dived in full when he renovated the place.

Nothing looked as it had when she lived here, yet she still heard the memories of her and her sister laughing and giggling as they raced down this hallway. When she got too close to the pain she stopped thinking and knocked on the door of the bedroom she used to call her own. "Lexie?"

Quiet rustling answered her.

She knocked and called louder.

"Leave me alone."

"Lexie, it's Maude. I came as I promised I would."

Maude waited. Sometimes a person needed to feel as though she had some control over her life, even if it was how long it took you to answer your door, or if you answered it at all.

"I have a few things for you." Nothing like a good bribe, Maude thought as she pressed her hand to the door.

Scrambling ensued, followed by a forceful yanking open of the door. Maude let her hand drop to her side and stepped back. "I'll come downstairs in a few minutes." The scowl on Lexie's face reminded her of Henry, and Maude's heart broke for both of them.

"I'll wait in the living room." Maude smiled to let her know she wasn't put off by the child's mood.

Inside the room, Maude could see carnage. Deflated stuffed animals and tufts of strewn fluff. A picture with Lexie, her father and Minnie Mouse lay on the floor, its glass shattered.

Lexie glared up at her in challenge.

Maude kept on the smile. "Take your time. I'm not in a hurry."

As Maude turned away, the door slammed behind her.

She made herself comfortable in the living room on the couch across from the cold but beautiful stone fireplace. The Persian rugs gracing the shining floors seemed a half-continent away from where they should be, and the lamps and ceiling fixtures of horns and antlers made her smile. Some clichés played well, especially when they were perpetrated by someone so full of life and adventure as Henry Daley had been.

Maude had finished one and a half copies of *Montana: the Magazine of Western History* by the time Lexie clomped down the stairs and into the living room. The girl plopped into the green leather lounge chair near where Maude sat on the couch.

After a few minutes of Lexie ignoring her, Maude got up and moved over to perch on the arm of the chair.

Lexie pushed up from the chair, took a couple of steps, and fell onto the couch, arms folded, lower lip out in a good pout. But Maude was not dissuaded. The child had come down to see her. She could easily have stayed in her room.

"Anger works," Maude said after a few moments more of silence.

Lexie made a sort of snorting noise. "What?"

"Anger sometimes helps keep me from falling apart when things go wrong."

"It's not fair." Lexie unfolded her arms and busied herself playing with the laces on the neck of her bright blue knit top. "He should still be here."

Maude wondered how many times Lexie had been offered platitudes like, *your father loved you* or *he didn't die on purpose*. "He should."

The girl's head snapped up and Maude continued. "He should have found a way to stay with you. He should have given up the high-adventure stuff and stayed here."

"He'd have been bored out of his mind."

Maude smiled at the sage observation of one so young.

"He was one of the most fun and exciting people I ever knew," she said quietly.

"Me, too. He could even beat Billy Harmon at snowboard racing. Do you think he—" Lexie stopped and put the end of the lace in her mouth.

"It's all right to ask anything you want."

Lexie bobbed her red curls up and down and her eyes watered. "Kelly thought we should just try to remember him as he was and not what he might have been like after."

"I don't know much about what happened except that he fell in Alaska." Maude knew little about the accident that had killed the handsome, young thrill seeker. She only knew she missed her friend terribly.

Lexie sat forward and put her elbows on her knees and her chin in her hands. "Why didn't you marry him? You could have kept him safe, and you'd have made an all right mom."

Maude moved over to the couch. "What do you suppose he would say to you if he came back to see you?"

When Maude sat down, Lexie snuggled against her. Maude held still, afraid to move, afraid to spook this child who found human contact so hard to accept.

"I think he would say, 'Sorry, Lexie. I didn't mean to leave you.'" Lexie's voice hitched as she spoke. "Sometimes he did things without thinking them through very well."

Maude wanted to wrap her arms around the child and offer comfort, or at least take her hand and put a kiss on it, the way she saw Sally do when one of her children was feeling the pain the world inflicted. But Lexie had been let down so many times by so many people, she had to protect herself somehow.

"I don't want to love him anymore," Lexie continued. "It hurts too much."

"I loved him, too. I still do because I can't forget him."

"I wish you could come and live here with us." Lexie slid away. Despite her words the moment of closeness was over.

Maude smiled. "Living here would be difficult to arrange."

"I could help."

Maude wished it were that easy to mend nearly mortal wounds.

GUY ROUNDED THE CORNER of the barn slightly faster than he should have, and the tires skidded on the gravel. When he brought the truck back into control, he glanced up to spot Maude's Subaru parked outside the ranch house. The fatigue fled and the emotions that replaced the dog-tiredness were unexpected. He wanted to kiss her again, and he wasn't as sorry as he should be for feeling that way.

He parked the truck in the barn and headed for the house.

Maude had come to chew him out about treating the kid last night. He could take that, deserved it even.

In the mudroom, as he cleaned off some of the dust, the indistinct sound of female voices floated out from the living room. Maude must have coaxed Lexie from her room.

He didn't think it was all that unreasonable for him to refuse to let a child buy makeup or to tell her she was not going "out to meet friends" with Bessie's seventeen-year-old daughter, but Lexie did. *The only friend I have from Montana is in California visiting her grandparents,* she had shouted as if that explained everything. Then she had stormed off to her room and refused to come out. Nearly drove Bessie to distraction.

The child needed someone she trusted, someone who was there just for her, and right now, like it or not, that person was Maude. He'd give her another chance. He wished he had been given another chance at being a better brother to Henry.

He dried his face and started through the kitchen.

"Maybe if I gave the ranch back to you. It's mine, you know. Dad left it to me." When he heard Lexie's words, Guy halted as if he'd hit a wall.

"Lexie, this is a great place to live," Maude said slowly as if choosing her words carefully. "I thought I'd live here the rest of my life."

The longing in her voice was unmistakable. So she wanted the ranch back. Maybe if she couldn't get it through the father, she thought she'd get it from the daughter. The sane side of Guy said not to jump to conclusions. The side that rose to protect his younger brother's child said to march in and toss her out.

"It sucks here. Uncle Guy treats me like a kid."

When he stepped through the doorway, the two of them were on the couch facing away. He watched Maude almost stroke the wild red curls and then pull back. "Did you talk to him about it?"

"He thinks if he doesn't give me rules, I'll go play in traffic, or get hit by a falling rock, or drink poison, I don't know."

Maude chuckled at the adolescent hyperbole. "Why do you suppose he's like that?"

Lexie stretched back and probably rolled her eyes at Maude. He had gotten that look from her many times already.

"Because he thinks I'm still a baby."

"I brought you something." Maude handed Lexie a bag from Taylor's Drugstore. "I hope this helps."

She took the bag from Maude and crumpled it against her the way she probably held her teddy bear not that long ago.

"Why do you suppose he really didn't want me to have makeup? I don't see how it could hurt."

"Maybe you should ask him." Guy strode into the room.

Lexie and Maude each had a look of innocent surprise on her face. *Yeah, right.* He wanted to grab the bag from Lexie, but he wanted to have that discussion in private, not two on one.

"Lexie, there's a phone call for you." Bessie stood in the doorway holding a handset out toward the girl.

"See ya." She waved and bounded from the room clutching the bag as if it held gold bullion.

Bessie stayed in the doorway frowning.

"What's wrong, Bessie?" Guy asked.

"It was the Kearney boy from the next ranch. He's older than she is and I don't like him."

A boy. Now, what was he supposed to do with that? "I think we can let her have a phone conversation." He shoved a hand through his hair and hoped he was doing the right thing.

Bessie left, shaking her gray head and clucking.

Maude got up and approached him. "We need to talk."

When she stopped next to him, her scent spun a shock of desire through him; he wanted to kiss her until she couldn't stand. "Too many ears here. Let's take a walk."

The fresh air would also help clear his head.

Outside they walked silently down the century or so old road that led toward the wild heart of the ranch. Ahead a bridge of thick planks crossed over a stream. On the other side of the bridge a stand of pine trees seemed ancient and endless.

While the terrain on one side of the road fell gently into a shallow valley, on the other side trees and boulders climbed a steep slope. A few miles or so farther than the bridge, where the ranch abutted the state forest, stood an old hunter's cabin outfitted for survival should a winter storm strand someone. Lexie had asked to stay there some night. Said it sounded "so romantic," as if she knew about such things.

The sun had dropped behind the mountains, but the sky had not yet started to glow pink. The diffuse light made shadows of mystery behind every tree.

Guy had to admit, if he had grown up here, he wasn't sure there could be any reason why he wouldn't want it back. He thought of the ring. Apparently it had been her grandmother's, but that's all Bessie or Jake knew.

He chanced a look at Maude. She walked along, hands in the pockets of her jacket. The muted afternoon light made her hair shine a soft brown and gave a delicate glow to her skin. No doubt Maude DeVane was a desirable woman.

If they were in Chicago, and had just met, he would explore that for what it was. Here in this tiny corner of civilization and with the delicate mental health of a child involved, things were more complicated. He should not have kissed her five years ago and for sure not last night.

That didn't stop him from wanting to touch her, to stroke her hair.

She paused to lean on the horizontal trunk of a gnarled, old tree that sat on the edge of where the land fell steeply into the valley.

When he stopped beside her, she eyed him from head to toe. He was ready. He had been wrong, he'd say so, and that should settle things quickly.

"How could you bury your talent and skill on a ranch?"

Choking anger rose swiftly and sharply. "What I was and what I did in the past is no longer relevant," he said, holding his tone emotionless, surprised by how strong his feelings were that wanted to burst free.

"It was relevant to the Thompson boy." She spoke kindly.

"I don't want your understanding." He kept his voice level. "No one here was ever going to find out I practiced medicine."

"They know now."

"They know now." He echoed her words, and his life could change as quickly as Montana weather—again.

Her eyes glistened a rich russet as she stared at him and waited. How could a face like that hide calculating duplicity? He wanted to kiss her soft lips, to hold her in his arms. Make him forget there were things he could not heal.

MAUDE PUSHED OFF the tree to face Guy. There was something in his face she had never seen in him before. Vulnerability. The steel-cold man who could reportedly call the shots to save a life better than most looked as if that path had been shaken for him.

True, his brother had died, but there must be something more to it to have driven him away from medicine. The way he still bristled with anger made her believe she had gotten close.

"What don't I know about you?" she asked.

"How's the sheriff?" A clear deflection of the question she asked.

"He'll be all right. But I didn't come here to discuss any patient, except Charlie."

"There isn't an excuse for what I did." He glanced at her for a moment and then turned to gaze out over the valley.

The openness on his face didn't hide the pain his short answer seemed to cause him. *What secrets are you hiding, Doctor?*

Secrets. The malevolent ones ate at you from the inside, and the longer you kept them the more deeply they burrowed into your soul.

Pink light invaded the valley before them. The sky had been this color when she lost her mother's ring and set a desperate sequence of events in motion.

"Maude?" He said her name quietly, as if he knew he was disturbing her.

She shook the webs of old memories from her brain and shifted her gaze to meet his. "I should ask you if you left medicine or were driven out, but I'll settle for—are you licensed in the state of Montana?"

"I am. Since Henry first made this his base of operations."

"Don't treat patients at my clinic without my permission." Liability aside, she would need to check out the integrity of his credentials. "There's a big-city, E.R. doctor on a ranch in Montana dealing with the likes of Cynthia Stone."

Slowly, deliberately, she turned away. Let him be mad.

*Seminar leader* popped into her head, and she glanced back at him. He looked annoyed and she started to laugh. She wasn't even sure why, but suddenly it was funny.

The whole damn world seemed funny. She gazed out over the valley and laughed some more.

She faced him again, and he stared at her as if she had a screw loose, and she laughed harder. "She calls you a 'seminar leader' as if it's a lower form of life, somewhere just beneath amoeba." The words came out in bursts.

He raised his eyebrows. "I expected several different kinds of angry from you, but all I get is—" He paused. "Ridicule?"

"You should be used to that by now, Mr. Leader." She laughed so hard, she collapsed back against the tree trunk and doubled over to grab her stomach.

Swiftly she felt herself being drawn away from the tree trunk. Guy pulled her upright.

"Stop that," he commanded and shook her gently.

She grinned at him and then everything stopped. Gently he drew her body against his. This time she pressed her palms into the hard plane of his chest.

She stared into the dark eyes. The small white scar at the corner of his eyebrow seemed angrier, newer than she had previously thought. When she reached up to touch it he covered her hand with his.

With her hand against his cheek and his hand on hers, he studied her face. When he peered into her eyes, his seemed to reflect the hunger inside her. And then she deeply inhaled the combined scent of pine and man as he slowly lowered his mouth to hers.

When their lips touched, raw need flared and all she could feel was his mouth moving over hers, her own body pressing as she snaked her arms around his neck to bring them closer together.

The feelings building inside her flashed and ignited the flame low in her belly. She wanted this.

He obliged, reaching out with his tongue to taste her. When he did, she pressed tighter against him and could feel his desire pressing against her.

Giggling and squealing penetrated the fog of emotion in Maude's brain, and she jumped away. No sooner than she had moved back, Lexie and Bessie's daughter careened around the bend in the road and raced across the bridge toward them.

"We gotta get a dip in before the sun goes down," Lexie shouted.

Maude looked at Guy. The waterhole in the stream was deep and cold and would be dangerous when the sun truly set. The alarm must have shown in her face because he said, "I know I should debate that, but I'll follow them down and make sure it's a quick dip."

"And I'm going to run away before we decide to debate what we were doing here."

He grinned and she desperately wanted another kiss.

"SALLY, can you talk?" Maude adjusted her phone's headset to a more stable position as she drove sensibly toward town. The more distance she put between herself and Guy Daley, she reasoned, the saner her thought processes would get.

"Oh, you sound excited. Yes. Yes, I can. Sweetheart, come and be bath monitor, please," Sally called to her husband and then came back on the line. "Don't go away."

There was a pause, some muffled conversation, then, "Okay, dish."

"I love how subtle you are, Sally."

"Subtle. You kiss Guy Daley in the middle of downtown and you have the nerve to call me subtle?"

"I enjoyed it, too, so I did it again today."

"What? Tell me. Tell me about kissing the enemy."

"Oh, Sally. I feel so ridiculous."

"You sound happy."

"Well, I am happy—that I'm still capable of having feelings for a member of the opposite sex."

"And there's something wrong with that?"

"There's something wrong with having feelings for Guy Daley."

"Other than he's the enemy…from the past I might add," Sally said pragmatically.

"Other than, he treated me like devil spawn for years—"

"The past, girlfriend, the past."

"And he's the person who can ruin my chances of proving to this valley that I can do the job."

"But you don't need to prove anything to this valley of slightly backward minds."

"I do. If I prove it to them, then…I…can prove it to myself." Maude realized as she said them, the words were true.

"Ah, there's the rub. But that's not his fault."

"Everything else is."

Sally laughed. "It's always their fault. I can't disagree with you there. So, fairy tales aside, what do you want to happen?"

"I wish I knew. There's something he's not talking about. I don't think it's anything about his ability to practice medicine or I'd have to have the deputy run him out of town for sewing up Charlie Thompson's head."

"I heard about the sheriff, too. Good job, Dr. DeVane. And like you have no secrets yourself."

"You know them."

"Most of them. Want to tell me the rest?"

# CHAPTER SIX

"SOMEDAY, I'll let you worm all my secrets out of me, but not today," Maude said to Sally.

"I'm going to hold you to that. But, suppose you and Dr. Daley fess up your secrets and they aren't so bad?"

"Well. All I know is I don't know what I feel. I've spent so long ignoring and being ignored, switching gears is hard. I do know one thing."

"Tell me, but be brief. They're getting loud and my husband is going to be overwhelmed any moment."

"I want to kiss him some more."

"Hmm. Just kiss?"

"Well—"

"Mommy." Maude heard the loud, sharp scream.

"Whoa. I gotta go. See you at the ice-cream social tomorrow."

"The social. No, wait. There can't still be a party. Doc's gone."

"It wasn't just a going-away party for Dr. Avery. It was also a welcome party for our new doctor. Surprise!"

"Oh God, Sally, will anybody come?"

Sally guffawed. "Seven Sandersons will be there. Your parents. Maybe Barry Farmington because there arc lampposts in the town square. People will come—because the town council voted to buy the ice cream for the occasion. Now go home and get some sleep. Tomorrow is your day off, and you get to spend the afternoon with your admirers."

After Sally hung up, Maude squeezed the silent phone in her hand. Would Guy Dalcy be there?

Was she crazy to think of Guy as anything but a stumbling block in her new life?

Was she crazy to want more from him?

Was she going to drive over the edge and into oblivion?

She sat up and jerked on the wheel to bring the car around the curve safely. That was close. No matter how bad it got, oblivion was not in the plan.

SEVERAL HOURS LATER when sleep didn't come, Maude sat on the window seat in her dark kitchen and stared out past the scrawny mountain birch into the deeply shadowed forest behind her home. A chill had her pulling her utilitarian robe tightly around the short ice-blue chiffon chemise she wore when she needed a bit of bolstering.

She liked the sheer chiffon. Sally had given it to her. *Mine keeps me motivated and proud of what I've got,* Sally had said.

Maude leaned back against the wall, closed her eyes and willed herself to get sleepy.

A few minutes ticked by and the rattling of her back door brought her alert.

Maude sat very still in the silence and listened. When the sound did not repeat, she allowed her tensed muscles to relax. The wind must have rattled the old aluminum storm door. Since it needed to be replaced, she hadn't bothered to take out the glass and put in the screen. Montana's wind often rattled the old thing.

She started to get up and, at a new sound, froze on the edge of the window seat. The handle of the inside door turned slowly, so slowly, she thought it might be the paranoia she had brought back from the big city.

Okay, this was St. Adelbert, she assured herself. A kid was probably sneaking into the wrong house.

When the door latch cleared the strike plate, she lowered her feet to the floor. Before she had a chance to push up to stand, the phone on the wall began to ring.

"Sheesh!" she hissed into the darkness.

She ignored the loud jangle of the phone and sidled into the sheltered corner beside the refrigerator. Maybe the sound would frighten the intruder away. She pulled her robe closed over the chiffon.

The phone stopped after the fourth ring, and she heard her own voice requesting the caller to leave a message or dial the emergency number. The machine clicked off during the silence that followed. The emergency service would field the call and contact her if necessary.

The door opened a crack.

Okay, time to panic just a little. She took her mobile phone from her pocket. St. Adelbert's or not, it was time to call the deputy on duty. When the phone in her hand began to ring, she nearly dropped it.

The door closed quietly.

*Whispering Winds,* the caller ID read.

She opened her phone.

"Is Lexie there?" Guy Daley demanded before she even had a chance to say hello, but the question relieved the anxiety she couldn't keep from building inside her.

"She might be." So much for needing the deputy.

"What's that supposed to mean?"

"It means someone was just trying to sneak in my back door." Her own anger flared and she stepped out from the alcove to peek through the window. What she could see of the porch was empty. "And if you'll be patient, I'll check."

Maude crossed the kitchen and flung open the back door. Sitting in the old wooden porch swing was a child with a mop of raggedy red curls.

"She's here."

"How could you—" Guy started, but Maude silenced the phone against her chest. She motioned Lexie inside and pointed to the window seat. When the child curled up on the cushion, Maude stepped out onto the back porch and closed the door.

"How could I lose a child?" She reined in her rising anger and tried to make it sound like a jest.

"How did she get into town?" he demanded. She wondered why he was trying to give some of the blame to her.

"Is this the child who made it from Chicago to Montana on her own?" Anger seeped into her tone. What had happened to make Lexie flee?

"Is she all right?"

"She looks physically fine. Why is she here?"

"She might not have run away at all if you hadn't brought that stuff to her and filled her head with ideas."

Clearly there were two Guy Daleys: the one she kissed a few hours ago and the one on the phone. She wanted to ask him to bring out his alter ego, but was certain that wouldn't be met with a very positive response.

Then she wondered how the bath salts and body oil she had given Lexie would encourage a child to run away. "What ideas?"

"I'll be right there to get her."

"No." Maude had released a child into suspect circumstances when she let Sammy McCormack go home with his father. She would not abandon Lexie to the unknown if she could help it. "It's the middle of the night. I'll bring her in the morning."

"I'll be there within the hour." His statement brooked no protest she might have wanted to give.

She gave him directions to her house, he said goodbye and the phone went silent in her hand.

"So how mad is he?" Lexie, the dear twelve-year-old Maude knew her to be, peeked from behind the door.

"How mad should he be?" Maude hadn't realized how cold she was until she stepped into the warm kitchen.

"Well, I don't really care." The twenty-something Lexie strode back to her perch on the window seat as if she were in total control.

"He's doing his best." Maude flipped on the light over the stove. She hoped Guy's best was good enough. "He's never had to act like a parent before."

"He stinks at it."

"That's not a very nice thing to say about your uncle." Maude wanted to push the curls away from Lexie's face. "He's on his way into town to get you."

Lexie turned and pressed her forehead to the glass. "I don't feel safe at the ranch."

"You feel frightened?" Maude stepped up beside Lexie to try to see her face. Fear. This was a wrinkle she hadn't considered.

"I feel— Yeah, I feel, I feel scared." She didn't turn away from the glass.

"Tell me what you mean." A feeling of dread spread through Maude. Of all the things she expected from this girl, "scared" was not one of them. Anger, rebellion, acting way too old for her age, but not fear. Come to think of it, she had never seen Lexie afraid, even at the prospect of climbing sheer rock walls or hang gliding with her father.

Alarms began to buzz inside Maude's head. "Tell me what's frightening you."

"I don't want to talk about it." She shifted toward Maude leaving behind a forehead print on the glass.

"At least tell me if there's anything I can do about it."

"Let me live here with you." Lexie crossed her arms over her chest as if to emphasize the challenge she had just hurled.

Maude had fallen into that one. "Lexie, I can't take you away from your uncle Guy."

"I just don't feel safe."

"Did one of the executives approach you, harm you?"

"They're too old and creepy to go near."

The alarms reached a frantic peak. "Did your uncle do anything to make you scared?"

Lexie laughed. "He tries, but he's not as mean as he thinks he is."

The klaxons abated a bit. "Life at the ranch will never be the same as it was when your father was alive."

Lexie nodded. "That's what I'm afraid of."

"Is going back to Chicago to live with Kelly and your brother an option?"

"I just get in the way with the baby there. She doesn't want to be bothered with me anymore."

And baby makes three wasn't meant to be without the father, Maude thought. "What about your grandparents?"

This time, she screwed up her face in disgust.

"I'm tired. I want to sleep until Uncle Guy gets here."

"I'm here whenever you want to talk."

"Can I sleep now?"

Maude showed her upstairs to the bed she had not been able to sleep in tonight and covered her with the quilt.

Downstairs again, she ground a couple handfuls of beans and made some coffee for the wait. After twenty minutes or so, she checked Lexie to find her fast asleep.

Good, because when her uncle arrived she had a thing or two to say to him, and she didn't want the child involved.

Sooner than she expected, lights from a vehicle filled the side yard, and then Guy Daley, dressed in jeans with a denim jacket over a sexily taut golf shirt, filled her doorway.

She restrained the hand that wanted to fly to her chest to still the hasty beating of her heart. Mad or not, Guy Daley had a way of breaking her focus and turning a good argument into meaningless garble and barely disguised panting.

They stared at each other silently, he standing and she at the kitchen table with her hands wrapped around a cup of cooling coffee. The dark mysteries in his eyes seemed deeper in the wee hours of the morning, and from the tenseness in his shoulders, it appeared as if he were holding back an explosion.

She checked to see that her old robe was securely tied and stood to meet him. "Why is Lexie here? What's happening at the ranch?" She moved around the table and stopped closer to where he stood.

"How can you put such ideas in her head? Isn't she confused enough?"

She took a step toward him about to ask him what he was talking about. Instead she asked, "So are we having another walk?" As soon as the words left her lips, she wanted them back. She raised her fingers to her mouth remembering the kiss.

He glared at her and she almost laughed. She knew he was remembering it, too.

"Where is she?"

"Upstairs asleep."

He drilled her with that look he must have used to intimidate many an uncooperative patient. No walk this morning, she guessed. But she couldn't help but think of the other Guy Daley, the touch of his hand, the heat of his breath on her cheek.

He placed a bag from Taylor's Drugstore on the counter, but didn't speak.

"If you're waiting for me to confess something, I can't think of anything to tell you," she said after a few moments.

He made a sound of disbelief. "You know I told her she couldn't have makeup."

"Yes, she told me." And Maude knew she probably should care, but she didn't want to think about makeup right now. She wanted to put her hands on his chest and go from there.

"She needs a chance to be a child, and sneaking out to be with an older boy is not it."

"She sneaked out to meet that boy on the next ranch?"

"You can't be surprised she did. I also took away the bag of stuff you gave her." His gaze challenged her.

She challenged back. "I don't see how—"

He took the bag he had placed on the counter and unceremoniously dumped the contents. Mascara, a bright shade of lipstick, eye shadow, eyeliners and several other items flew and skittered. One small tube of dark red something landed on the floor at her feet. He picked it up and looked at it.

"Bite Me?" He pointed the tube at her. "What kind of thing is this for a child?"

"Lip stain, I believe. You think I gave these to her?"

"She told me you did, and I saw you. Remember?"

Maude couldn't bring herself to point her finger at the sleeping child upstairs. She'd talk to Lexie first.

"She thought she might feel more like herself if she had makeup." Maude passed on what Lexie had said even if it was a bit misleading.

"You had no right. She needs stability in her life, not advice from anyone who feels like offering it. How could you tell her it was all right to see a boy who is four years older than she is?"

She did that, too? I really am a bad person, she thought. "She's trying to find where she fits in, to find friends out here."

"She's going about it the wrong way." He seemed as if he wanted to rant. He must be calling all of his professional control into play.

"She said you stink at being a parent."

For a second, she was sure he would explode. Then he relented and looked chagrined. "She's most likely right about that."

He stepped up close to where she stood, close enough for her to catch the seductive scent of an outdoors man; acquired, she guessed, since he left the city. The errant lock of his hair had fallen over his forehead and she wanted to brush it back, and she wanted to put her hands on his strong chest, to feel the strength of his heartbeat.

"It's brave of you to take on a child."

"She deserves for someone to try."

His dark eyes studied her until she knew she had to do something or feared she might expire from the anticipation.

"I'll get her." She forced the words out and started toward the living room.

"Maude."

She stopped and slowly spun. With his gaze locked to hers, he closed the gap between them and kissed her.

She opened her mouth for him to take what he wanted. His tongue explored, stroking hers as his hand moved a trail of heat up her side, skimming along the edge of her breast to her neck, lighting a fire in her body. He paused for a moment and then placed a trail of hot kisses along her jaw and down to the V formed by the overlap of her old robe. *Touch me. Touch me.* She almost cried the words aloud.

Then he lifted his head and with his other hand, reached inside her robe and slid his palm over the chiffon covering her already rigid nipple. She gasped with pleasure and pressed against his hand.

When he lifted her against him, she reached under his jacket and put her arms around his body. She stroked the rippling muscles of his back, unable, unwilling to check her actions.

He covered her mouth with his again and didn't give her a chance to breathe as he invaded her body and soul.

And then—with a deep groan, he pushed her gently away.

Hurt flared at his rejection.

"We can't do this. There is too much between us and there is Lexie to think about. We will only confuse her more."

His rational words assuaged the selfish hurt. She could not reasonably debate the issue of confusing an already floundering child. Still, his logic didn't quiet the roaring inside her head.

She wanted to reach out and draw him back to her.

Just then the door between the kitchen and the living room popped open and Lexie appeared. She looked between Maude and Guy a couple times of and then wordlessly walked out of the house.

TWENTY MINUTES LATER, Guy glanced at the child in the passenger seat feigning sleep. Henry had no right to leave her.

Maude DeVane was not good for her. She had not been good for his brother and she certainly was not good for him. And if Lexie had not been there, he wouldn't have stopped himself from taking what she offered. On so many levels he should not be attracted to Maude, but after tonight, he couldn't deny it.

He could, however, do something about it. He could keep his hands and all other parts of his body off her.

"GET UP. Get up. Get up, you slug-a-bed."

Maude opened her eyes and blinked up to see Sally standing over her grinning with mischief. "I came to make sure you came to the party."

"Go away. The party's not until two o'clock."

"It's twelve thirty-two."

Maude sat up and rubbed her face.

"Let them eat ice cream without me." She plopped back down, and pulled the covers over her face.

Sally tugged at the quilt to reveal Maude's head. "That's not how to win friends and influence people."

"They probably won't even miss me."

"The gossip sisters are sure to be at an ice-cream social no matter what the occasion. There's always gossip to be had or made if need be."

Maude laughed. "You are so mocking such nice old ladies."

Sally patted her arm. "Nice and nosy, and you don't want to disappoint them. Your parents'll be there—eventually. There'll be a huge crowd, somewhere up in the double digits."

"Let's see." Maude did her best to look disheartened. "Including the Sanderson family, my folks, the gossip sisters and Barry Farmington that would be about, what? A dozen? Most of you will be there for the free ice cream anyway."

"I know that's why I'm going."

"If you came to cheer me up, it's working. See." Maude put on a big silly grin and ducked back under the covers.

"Get up and get in the shower."

"Maybe I changed my mind. I don't want to be the new doctor. I just want to find a husband and have some kids."

"Be very, very careful what you wish for on that one. Besides, Dr. DeVane, you'd shrivel up in a ball if you didn't practice medicine."

Under the covers in the muted daylight, Maude knew Sally was right. She needed to practice medicine and she needed to do it right here in this valley.

She shoved the quilt away. "I never thought much about having a family until I saw you with yours. When I see what a good job the class goofball is doing, I start to think I might be able to pull it off."

Sally made a rude face at her and they both laughed.

"Well, just don't be in too much of a hurry." Sally sat on the edge of her bed. "If we had ten children between us, we'd have no time to visit."

"But they're so cute."

"Yeah? Try them 24/7 and see what you think. They're still cute, but only about seventy-five percent of the time. It's the other twenty-five percent that's a killer. Hey, I hear by way of the grocery store, you had a visitor during the night." Sally looked goo-goo-eyed at her.

Maude laughed again. "I had two."

"Ah, they sneak in pairs after we're all in bed. So that's how you can seem to go so long without a man."

"One was a twelve-year-old girl."

"Lexie?"

Maude nodded. "And her uncle Guy had to come and fetch her."

"Oh, yeah! And?"

"Why do you always think there's more?"

"Because with you two there always is."

"I get such mixed signals from him. One minute he's accusing me of being a bad influence on his niece and the next he's kissing me senseless."

"Senseless is good."

"Not for me it isn't."

"So what do you want to do?"

"I want to practice medicine in the valley for the rest of my life. I want the people here to think I do a good job and

I want a nice, uncomplicated man who will help me raise children—and do the cooking. I hate cooking."

Sally stood and put her hands on her hips. "All in good time. Right now, I want to go to a party and eat ice cream. Get in the shower."

"Don't you have to go home and do kid things?"

"And leave you here by yourself? No way. I left my husband with strict orders to get them all in their party clothes and get them to the square on time. It's so funny when he has to do things like that. Makes him glad to go back to the store on Monday. My job, right now, is to keep you from chickening out."

"Bawk. Bawk." Maude flapped her arms like wings.

"Get up."

It wasn't long before the two of them were in Sally's car on the way to the town square, because Sally said, "You'll have too many opportunities to run away and hide if we walk."

Maude was surprised to see fifty or so people already in the square when they arrived. She didn't know whether to be happy or not because she didn't know whether they were there to welcome her or to invite her to move on. The safety-in-numbers thing could make it go either way, and she had no true sense of which way the wind was blowing.

A welcome banner hung between two trees along the edge of the square. Another banner bid goodbye to the parting physician and his wife. A hastily added message bid the Averys congratulations on the birth of their first great-grandchild. The local news crew was taking pictures of groups under the banner. By dinnertime the Averys would have digital copies.

*They're a good bunch*, Sheriff Potts had said of the

people in the valley. Maude believed that, or she wouldn't still be here.

The gossip sisters, the ones responsible for most of the grocery store tidbits, were the first to greet Maude and Sally.

Sally stepped in front of Maude to take the first salvo.

"Mrs. Sanderson, how nice to see you. How are all those children?"

Sally smiled politely. "Hello, Cora. Hello, Ethel. It's nice to see the two of you someplace besides the other side of the canned peas display."

Maude wanted desperately to giggle at Sally's comment, but held it to a small, doctorlike smile.

"Dr. DeVane, welcome back to our humble town," Ethel said and two gray heads smiled at her.

"I'm so glad to be here. How are you ladies doing? We haven't had a chance to talk."

The two women might have been made from the same family mold, but for all they looked alike, they were not related. One was adopted from back east in the thirties and the other born here the same year, or at least, that's the way gossip had it.

"Ethel has a bit more rheumatism and I don't see quite as well, but Doc Avery kept us up and going."

If Maude wasn't mistaken, Cora had just delivered a challenge. Okay, that was fair. They weren't saying "get out of town," and she knew she could prove to them that she'd do the job well and with compassion.

"I hope to be able to do the same." Maude gave her best benevolent smile.

"So do we, dear." Ethel's tone was not entirely convincing, but after a moment, the two of them hurried away.

Sally leaned toward Maude and whispered. "Ice cream."

Maude elbowed her in the ribs and Sally giggled.

"You're just glad your husband is having trouble with the kids. You get to play footloose."

"At a party in the middle of the St. Adelbert town square with the gossip sisters in close attendance, I'm sure to have a high time."

"Too late." Now it was Maude's turn to do the elbowing.

Sally's children had spotted her. They screamed as one and sprinted toward their mother, the twins dragging identical blankets behind them in the grass.

"It's so good to be wanted," Sally said as she bent down to scoop the eldest and fastest into her arms.

"Yeah," Maude said quietly to herself.

While Sally greeted her children, Maude moved away and sought out a friendly face to say hello to. Two hours. If she could just get through the next two hours. The huge clinic in Chicago, where she was just another M.D., didn't seem quite so bad.

"Dr. DeVane."

"Barry Farmington." She almost laughed as she looked for his lamppost. His hands were empty and he stood alone. "It's nice to see you."

"Good to see you, too. This town could use some more good-looking women."

At least he hadn't called her Maudie. "Why, thank you, Barry. Have you had any ice cream yet?"

"I was just headed there. It's free, you know."

She smiled. "I know."

"Dr. DeVane," a woman's voice called from the distance.

Maude spotted Bessie trundling toward her. Her daughter followed. Lexie and Guy were close behind.

Maude's breath caught in the throat. She wondered when the next flight left for Chicago.

Guy nodded politely, Bessie's daughter ignored her and the twenty-something version of Lexie sans makeup gave her a look of mild disdain and major disinterest.

Bessie eyed Maude then Guy a couple of times and eventually stepped up to Maude.

"Welcome. Welcome. I thought we should come to show our support." Bessie gave Guy a pointed look and then hugged Maude. "It's so nice of the town to throw you a party."

Maude hugged and then stepped back. "It is, isn't it?" She glanced over Bessie's shoulder at Guy. Dressed in a dark blue golf shirt and slacks, he looked every bit as good as he did in denim. Forget the ice cream. She wanted to lick him and wanted him gone, too. He raised such confusing emotions in her.

Bessie's daughter tugged on her mother's arm.

"Well, I promised the girls ice cream." Bessie smiled.

When another group approached her, Guy turned away.

The deputies and their wives greeted her with smiles. And as the afternoon wore on, many people who had been to her office and many more that she had not seen since coming back to the valley came up to shake her hand, some with smiles and some with grim looks of doubt and reservation.

Some didn't approach her at all. They did approach the people scooping out the ice cream. And no one outright asked her to leave. That was good.

"Hello, dear," Maude's mother called, and her parents hurried toward her. Late as always, but here. She hugged both of them, prepared for the usual skepticism from her mother.

"What a nice turnout," her mother said pleasantly without a hint of amazement.

"Yes, I'm glad you made it." Maude smiled at her and wondered if her mother was getting used to the idea of her being the valley's doctor.

"What nice flowers they planted around the flagpole this year." Her mother pointed. "Not like that first year when they had such a fight about it. Oh, and I have the samples in the trunk."

Maude rolled her eyes at her father. Samples for the carpet, draperies, bedding, paint and anything else her mother could think of. Her father smiled and flicked his eyebrows.

"How's Amanda?" Maude asked.

"She's fine," her mother replied and quickly added, "We thought it would be too much to bring her, dear."

"Blanche, oh, Blanche," someone called and, at the sound of her name, Maude's mother waved.

"We'll be at your house in a little bit." Maude's mother tugged her father's arm to come with her and to visit old neighbors and friends gathered around the ice-cream scoopers. Anything to keep from talking about Amanda.

Time had gone mercifully fast. There were still many people in the square and most seemed to be having a good time. Not bad. And a half hour and the party would be over.

Someone thrust a cup of vanilla ice cream with chocolate sprinkles on it in front of her.

"Yum," she said as she took the cup, and turned to see the ice-cream bearer was Guy Daley. Yum again. "Um— thank you."

"Just the person we need to talk to."

Maude and Guy turned to see Mr. McCormack and

another town council member. McCormack stepped between Maude and Guy, dragging the other man with him.

"Mr. McCormack," Guy acknowledged and took a half step away to try to include Maude.

"Well, Dr. Daley, are you ready to get started, or do you need a couple of weeks?" McCormack asked.

## CHAPTER SEVEN

MAUDE REALIZED she was gaping at the council members and alternately at Guy Daley in horror. Guy, at least, had the civility to toss an apologetic glance in her direction.

An apology for taking away her livelihood, her self-respect— She closed her mouth and turned away. Everything she had wanted since she was ten years old.

"Maude," Guy called after her.

Apology not accepted. She tossed the cup of ice cream in the trash can and did not turn back.

"Uncle Guy. Uncle Guy," Lexie hollered as Maude headed for the edge of the square. "You have to come over here, Uncle Guy."

To hell with Chicago, Maude thought. They were going to have to drag her kicking and screaming from this valley.

The town council members had been exercising their right to ask a new doctor to work in the valley. She didn't own the people after all. All she really had the right to was the clinic building and what went on inside.

She didn't have an innate right to the patients' hearts or any part of them. It should be that way. Whoever practiced medicine here had the responsibility to earn the respect of these people. In this valley that someone was going to be her.

As she walked, the afternoon breeze cooled her ire and her bravado began to fade. She hadn't thought she would have to win the valley by conquest, but it was war or the highway. She'd have to sharpen her spear.

She smiled as she trudged up her driveway, wondering if the town council sorely regretted that they were forced by Doc Avery's schedule to have his party and the annual picnic separately. They were going to have to buy ice cream twice, three times if they welcomed Dr. Daley with an ice-cream social.

She yanked open her back door and plopped down at the kitchen table. After staring for a while at the scrawny mountain birch that seemed to stand defiantly against the backdrop of the towering forest in her backyard, she pushed up and went to the window. "I'm going to watch you grow up," she said to the little tree and it answered her by happily dancing in the breeze.

Footsteps tread on her back porch. Must be her parents. They were good-hearted people. Maude knew she should appreciate her mother's efforts, and she was sure she would when things were all finished.

"Hello, Maudie dear," her mother greeted as she entered the back door followed by her husband heavily burdened with luggage and sample books.

"I was just about to make coffee. Do you want some?" She welcomed each to her home with a hug.

"No, thank you, dear. I'm going to get these samples ready for you to look at."

Her father kissed her on the head and gave her a sympathetic look. Then he followed his wife into the living room, carrying enough samples to make a patchwork quilt big enough to cover the entire house.

As Maude poured beans into the coffee grinder, an image popped into her head. One male doctor and two town councilmen hanged by their thumbs on the street corners of St. Adelbert. She smiled and pressed down to start the grinder whirring. She didn't know where the thought came from, but she liked it.

On the ground near the men were two buckets, one of snowballs and one of rotten tomatoes. A sign above the head of each man said, "Please hurl objects at these men only if they deserve it." The ground below each man was a veritable glacier of tomato sauce. And she saw herself standing over the buckets trying to decide which to throw next.

"Dear," her mother called from the living room, "do you think you can come here for a minute? I want to know which samples you like for the curtains and the couch."

"I'll be in as soon as the coffee's ready."

It had seemed like such a small thing, to relinquish control of decorating her home to her mother. But now—

A few minutes later, a cup of coffee in her hand, Maude pushed open the swinging door to the living room to the smiles of her mother and father. Actually her father took the opportunity to flee to the kitchen.

On the first set of samples for the sofa and chair, Maude tried, "you pick," and got a, "how can you not care?" On the second batch for the draperies she tried, "that one," and her mother's reply was, "that looks like something Cora or Ethel would have chosen."

Maybe her mother wasn't too old to be hung by her thumbs.

"I'm tired of samples." Maude knew her mother was going to pick whatever she wanted, no matter what Maude said.

"Oh, we have to look at them all, dear. I'll go upstairs

and see what I think first." With books and strips of cloth clutched to her bosom, her mother took off with a purpose.

"You could have saved us all a lot of trouble if you'd have married that Henry Daley fella." Maude looked up to see her father. "But since he's gone, why don't you go after his brother?"

"Dad, how strong are your thumbs?"

He looked at her and then held up his thumbs and flexed them. "Strong as any, I guess. Why do you ask?"

"Why do you say such a thing about me and the Daley brothers?"

"We'd all still be on the ranch and your mother wouldn't be pestering you about draperies."

She never could get her father to understand she and Henry were only friends. And she'd never told him she hadn't wanted to buy the ranch his great-great-grandfather had settled.

"I'd be in town setting up a medical practice."

"I still don't see what that's got to do with my thumbs."

"Never mind," she said to her father, and when her back doorbell rang, she excused herself. Who could be there? She'd seen just about everyone in town this afternoon.

What if it was Guy Daley? Her steps faltered. How could she look at him now?

She yanked the door open.

"Mr. Hawes," she said to the elderly man who stood on her stoop holding his hat in his hand. "Please come in. The deputy told me about your wife. I'm so sorry."

Since returning to the valley, Maude hadn't seen Ida Hawes. Dr. Avery had said she had end-stage Alzheimer's disease, but that her husband kept her at his side, rather than take her to a facility a hundred miles away.

She had Mr. Hawes take a seat at the table. He nodded when she asked him if he'd have a cup of coffee.

After taking a few sips, he looked up at her.

"Could I have saved Ida if I'd called you to come and see her, Dr. DeVane?" The pain of new loss strained his voice and etched his face. "I want you to tell me the truth, Doctor."

Old love, just like Sheriff and Mrs. Potts, Maude thought.

"I'm afraid there is no way to tell that for sure," she said kindly.

He put his hands in his lap and hung his head.

Though she could not see the tears, she knew he cried them. "Mr. Hawes, you couldn't have known. Even on her good days, she couldn't have told you she felt bad."

He shook his head but didn't look up.

"Doc said I should have taken her to Kalispell and put her in a home. She might still be alive if I had."

"She was sick for a long time, wasn't she?"

"Couldn't even yell at me for years now." He looked up and gave her a tiny, teary smile.

"I don't want to second-guess what Dr. Avery told you, but if it were me, I'd have done the same thing you did."

"But you're a doctor. You would have known something was wrong."

"I might have. Although when things are so close to home, doctors are people first. So it's possible I might not have known." She put a hand on his shoulder. "What I *would* have known was that every day she would have had someone at her side who loved her very much."

"Did I love her enough?" He pulled out a big red-and-white handkerchief and wiped at his eyes.

Maude smiled at him. "If someone loved me as much as you love her, I'd want him at my side all the time."

"Said she didn't want to be a burden, but I never thought of her that way. I just thought of her as the woman I loved who needed me."

"Considering everything, she had some good luck in her life."

"Because she met me?" He sounded uncertain, as if it was hard to believe he was anyone's good luck.

"I bet you did exactly what she would have wanted. What do you think she would have said?"

He laughed out loud. "Do you wanna know what she said to me over and over when she could still talk?"

"I do."

"'Do the dishes, you big lazy lout.'" He laughed again and wiped a tear with the handkerchief. "Guess I must not have done them enough when she could remember. I always figured that thought played over and over in her mind when she was still good, and when she was not so good, it was one of the things she could remember. And you wanna know what else she said?"

"Of course."

He leaned in and whispered, "'Come over here, you big lout, your Ida wants you.'"

His ears turned pink and he put his hand up to cover his mouth. "I don't know why I said that to you."

She smiled. "I do. You wanted to share about your life with Ida, so someone else would appreciate her the way you do."

His expression changed to thoughtful. "I think you're right."

Maude heard the kitchen door open. She looked up to see her mother and motioned for her to stay back.

"So what do you think would have happened if you had called me to come out to see her?"

"You'da come and she still would have died because there wasn't anything to do for her."

"She had good reason to love you, Mr. Hawes. You're a very understanding man."

"And you're a very understanding doctor."

Maude didn't get that lump in her throat very often in Chicago, but suddenly she was afraid she'd squeak if she spoke, so she nodded and smiled.

"Thank you, Dr. DeVane." He stuffed the handkerchief into his pocket, took his hat, and shuffled to the door. When he turned, he looked up. "Oh, hello, Mrs. DeVane."

"My sympathies, Mr. Hawes," her mother said.

He closed the door quietly behind him.

Maude prepared herself for the usual from her mother, but instead of saying anything, Blanche DeVane did the most unimaginable thing.

She turned and walked silently away.

Standing alone in the kitchen with her empty cup in her hand, Maude wasn't sure what that meant. Her mother was so free with her disapproval. Could it be Maude had done something well?

AFTER SUNRISE on Wednesday morning, while her parents slept, Maude made coffee, one of the reliable staples in her life. She had spent the past two mornings at breakfast with her mother, talking samples when Maude was lucky, and lack of husbands when she was not. Her smart father would duck out shortly after his last forkful of food for his *morning constitutional.*

Today Maude took a thermos of the freshly brewed

coffee and drove out of town toward Kalispell. In the last two days, between her parents, her patients and the utter exhaustion left to her at the end of the day, she had barely had time for her own thoughts. Away from home and town, she might get her head around a bit of peace and quiet. Bolster the nerves she'd need to face another day at the office, wondering how many more she'd have left if Daley and those council members had things their way.

She stopped her Subaru in a pullout used for winter safety and summer viewing. This was the countryside that fed her soul. Mountains soared high into the bright blue sky, endless dark green pines, aspens fluttering all summer and burning golden in the fall. She rolled down her window—and water burbled everywhere this time of year.

She laid her head back and let the early morning breeze blow across her face. The ice cream with the chocolate sprinkles she never ate at the social pushed into her mind, and with it came the memory of the bearer. She sat forward. Guy Daley's handsome face, his dark eyes, his athletic body. This was not peace.

She would have believed the cone was some sort of offering of conciliation, if Dr. Daley's duplicity had not been laid bare by the good men of the town council. She never thought of being beholden to Mr. McCormack, but he had opened her eyes.

A red pickup truck pulled in behind her tingeing her perfect view with a faint cloud of oily exhaust. A moment later a large shadow filled her window, and she looked up.

Jimmy Martin's anxious face peeked in at her. "Are you all right, Dr. DeVane?"

"I'm fine, Jimmy. Thank you for stopping to check. I came out here for the scenery before I went to work."

"Okay then. Have a nice day." He spun and sprinted away. "She's just lookin' at the scenery," he called to someone in the truck behind her.

Maude looked in her rearview mirror to see Curly Martin waving his pink cast at her. He looked even more cowboy with his hat on. She reached out the window and waved back. Although Jimmy sounded puzzled that someone would be out looking at the scenery, she was sure she had these two on her side. She smiled and thanked them for the dose of courage.

By quarter of eight, she was in the office ready to see her first patient. Charlie Thompson. His parents had scheduled a visit to have the boy checked. These were the "every duck in a row and at attention" kind of people. Logical people. A kind she was sure she could serve well.

When she pushed open the door to the exam room, Charlie looked up and started to cry. She smiled.

"Good morning, Mr. and Mrs. Thompson." She walked over to the boy. "Hi, Charlie. How's Bella today?"

The child cried harder and buried his face in his mother's chest. Sometimes the doggy worked and sometimes it didn't.

Maude went to the sink on the far side of the room and lathered her hands with soap. Charlie watched her carefully as she cupped and squeezed her hands until a large bubble popped out and sat on top of her thumbs. She held the bubble out. "Blow, Charlie."

The little boy blew on the bubble and it floated away toward his father who pretended to be afraid. Charlie giggled at his daddy's antics and then sat quietly against his mom.

When the exam was complete, Mrs. Thompson took Charlie from the room and Mr. Thompson stayed behind.

"Dr. DeVane, thank you for checking Charlie over." Mr. Thompson smiled politely. "We heard that the doctor who treated him wasn't a doctor from around here. We just wanted to make sure everything was all right, and no offense to you, that he was qualified and trained."

"Dr. Daley is qualified and had been practicing emergency medicine in Chicago for almost ten years before he came out here." Maude picked up the boy's chart from the counter.

"I'm going to be straight with you, Doctor. I heard you were leaving and Dr. Daley is going to be taking over. Now, I'm relieved to hear he is trained so well in the technical part of the job, but will he understand the folks around here?"

"Mr. Thompson, I don't really know what's happening with Dr. Daley. He hasn't shared his plans with me."

"But if you leave the valley… Well, we've found the place we want to raise our children and that included a doctor who knows the people here."

She wanted to give the man the assurance she would never desert this valley, and two weeks ago, she would have been able to do so. "I love this valley, too, Mr. Thompson."

"If there is anything we can do to keep you here—" he gave her an earnest look "—please let us know."

"Thank you." She wanted to hug him.

There was nothing more she could tell him, so she opened the door of the exam room for him to step out.

She was about to head into the next exam room when Arlene came hurrying up, the pencil behind her ear. "There's a phone call for you, Dr. DeVane."

"Can you take a message?"

"It's Dr. Daley. He said it's urgent."

"I'll take it in my office."

Maude rushed down the hallway and closed herself in her office.

"Is she with you again?" Guy's tone was strained but not terse.

"No. She isn't." Lexie missing again? Maude tried not to be alarmed.

"She left sometime before six o'clock this morning. She's not with any of the surrounding ranch families, and none of the deputies has found any leads."

*What have you done to that poor child? What reason did you give her to run away again?* If Maude could have reached through the phone and gotten answers, she would have done so.

"I hope you find her soon." *Please be safe, Lexie.* "Will you call me when you find her?"

The silence on the line spoke loudly, but then he said, "Yes, I'll call."

Maude had to force herself to concentrate on the people who had come to see her. A few sore throats. One failure-to-heal ankle strain and several people for checkups.

As the morning passed and there was no word about Lexie, she wanted to cancel her afternoon appointments and go to the ranch, but she couldn't do that to her patients.

She doubted there was anything she could do at the ranch, and being there would not ease her worry anyway. By the time the last patient left, she had convinced herself they must surely have found the child or she'd have heard something by now. She picked up the phone to call, but decided she'd drive out instead.

When Maude left the clinic, the deputy was standing

beside her car for the second time. He didn't look as if he'd come to give her good news this time, either.

"Hello, Deputy," she said cautiously as she approached.

"Dr. DeVane, they haven't found Lexie Daley yet."

"It's been more than ten hours."

"I came to see if you might know someplace on the ranch she could hide."

A cave came to mind. She remembered Lexie excitedly telling her about how she and her father had discovered a cave. Maude didn't tell the child she and Amanda used to call the place Desperado's Hideout.

"Why does Dr. Daley think she's still on the ranch?"

"She took a fanny pack with water bottles and her hiking boots are missing, so she might be." He shifted from foot to foot as he spoke.

"How long has he known this? Never mind." She waved a hand. It didn't matter that he might have wasted half a day. It only mattered what she could do now. "I might know of a place."

"Could you tell 'em over the phone how to get there?"

"It's a showing kind of thing, Deputy. I could tell them, but they'd still be looking when I got there."

"I'll drive you out there and back."

She looked down at her dress shoes. "I need to go home and change into something I can hike in. I'll drive myself."

GUY WATCHED as Maude's Subaru approached. He had spent the day vacillating between growing dread for Lexie's safety and an equally expanding disquiet at Maude's bad influence on the girl.

She stopped the car several feet from him and stepped

out wearing old jeans, a soft tan shirt tucked in at the waist and hiking boots. She'd come to help, and like her or not, the feelings of dread lessened a little at the sight of her.

Bessie rushed up and tearfully hugged Maude. "Thank you for coming, Dr. DeVane. It's going to be dark soon. I'm so afraid for our little girl."

"Yes, thank you for coming." Guy echoed the sentiments of his housekeeper.

Maude faced him when he spoke. He expected to see hate or loathing in her eyes, but all he found was concern.

"I'm ready to go whenever you are," she replied matter-of-factly.

"Jake's almost here. He was on his way to the airport in Missoula with the Mountain High people when we realized Lexie was missing."

"I suspect it nearly killed him not to be here," Bessie added.

When Maude didn't react, he noticed she was looking over his shoulder. He turned.

Two of the searchers on horseback rode out of the woods side by side. One of them shook his head, and as they approached Maude stepped forward to greet them.

Each man slung a leg over and slid from his horse to the ground as easily as most people stood up from a chair.

"Coleman Dawson." Maude reached out a hand to the tall, dark-haired cowboy whose anxious palomino stood at the ready behind him, a noble steed prepared to do whatever was asked and Guy suspected the same of the edgy-looking man.

"Ma'am." He shook her hand with a sad nod and then addressed Guy. "I have to go. My wife and daughter will be home soon and well—I'll be expected."

Guy didn't know what Cole's story was, but Bessie had been eager to say there was trouble of some kind over on the Lazy D Ranch.

"Thanks, Cole." Guy shook the man's hand. "We appreciate your help."

Cole nodded to Bessie and the other rancher and made to leave.

"And Baylor Doyle," Maude said to the second cowboy who was only a bit shorter and blond. His blue eyes twinkled at her and she smiled.

"So, Little Miss Maudie is now Dr. DeVane."

"And I see Little Bay Boy has grown up quite nicely." She poked his large bicep.

"I'll take that as an invitation to ask you out on a date," the cowboy drawled.

Maude grinned at him. "It's an invitation for a hug."

It didn't take the cowboy a second to respond and a moment later, he held Maude wrapped in a pair of strong arms, clasped against what Guy suspected was a stone-hard chest.

Baylor pulled back to look at her. "Still no date for you and me?"

"No date. I always told you, you're too young and too flirty for me."

Baylor grinned white teeth against tanned skin and a flash of pique made Guy want to tear the two of them apart.

"Where do you think Lexie might be?" Guy could not keep all the terseness from his voice.

Maude stepped away from the cowboy, the smile gone from her face. "There's a cave a few miles from here. If she's there, she's safe."

"A cave? Where? I've seen the records from the ranch. There isn't even anecdotal information about a cave." Guy knew he sounded harsh, but he felt beaten and raw.

"That doesn't mean it isn't there." Baylor Doyle took a step toward Guy, a menacing look on his face. Ranchers, men or women, stuck together, at least against the outside world.

Bessie stepped between the three of them. "Have you eaten, Dr. DeVane?"

Food seemed irrelevant, but Guy was sensitive enough, at least, to know it might be all Bessie thought she had to offer under the circumstances.

"I'm fine, Bessie." Maude put a comforting arm around the older woman's ample shoulders. "We'll find her. She'll be okay. She's a very smart girl."

Bessie's eyes teared up and she wiped her hands unnecessarily on her apron. "I hope so. I hope so."

As the housekeeper headed toward the house, Mountain High's blue van pulled into the yard in a cloud of dust. Jake sprang from the driver's seat as if he'd been ejected. "She's not back."

It wasn't hard to tell from their faces that the girl hadn't returned. Jake had vowed to get back as soon as he could get rid of Ms. Stone and the rest, and Guy knew him well enough to know that not being here had almost been enough to kill that cowboy.

Baylor shook Jake's hand. Neither man said a word.

Maude greeted Jake and then opened the trunk of her car. Inside were supplies and what he now recognized as a rescue pack. This one had a warm blanket tied to the bottom.

"She might have gone to a cave here on the ranch," Maude said to Jake who removed his cap and smoothed back his thick hair.

"There's been a rumor about a cave here, but I never found it," Jake said as he reached into her trunk for the pack.

Guy held a hand up toward Baylor and turned to Maude. "What makes you so sure there is a cave?"

"I've been there."

Hope sudden and bright sprang up in his chest. Guy wasted no time collecting flashlights and water bottles in carrying harnesses. He hoped the child was safely tucked away in this cave rather than somewhere on the road between here and Chicago.

"Let's go." Maude explained, "We can take the truck partway, and then we'll have to hike in."

"I have to be going, too," Baylor said as he tugged on a worn cowboy hat with a snakeskin hatband.

"Thanks for your help." Guy extended a hand to the man who stood beside an impatient brown-and-white paint.

"Good hunting. Call if you don't find her." Baylor tipped his hat to Maude and led his horse to the trailer.

Maude, Guy and Jake stowed their gear in the bed of the truck. They got into the vehicle, Jake driving, Maude in the middle.

"Take the logging road to where it forks for the hunter's cabin and park there." Maude spoke softly as Jake started out into the heart of the ranch.

The rough dirt road led past the barn between two tall hills, the one on the right covered with a stand of pine trees and the left one with grass, sage and a few early wildflowers.

Lexie was smart and resilient and he kept telling himself she'd be all right.

As they bounced along, Guy studied Maude's profile

while she stared at the road ahead. A curl of her soft brown hair swept down across her cheek and she kept pushing it back. He had to stop himself from reaching out to push it away for her.

Whenever the old logging road bounced the truck particularly hard, the contact between their thighs became almost intimate.

"How do you know about the cave?" He leaned closer to the door to keep contact to a minimum. He wasn't even sure he could trust her; he sure as hell shouldn't be hot for her.

"Grandfather brought my sister and I up here. He said it had been a sacred place. He told us if we told our parents or anyone else, people would overrun it." She smiled faintly.

"Sister?" He really did not know her.

"She lives in Great Falls now." Her voice stayed quiet, but held an underlying sadness, as though she was sad her sister lived so far away.

Jake glanced at the two of them, but his grim look of concentration did not change.

A sudden dread filled Guy. If Lexie crawled into a cave and some old rock formation crumbled on top of her, they might never find her. "When was the last time you were at the cave?"

"At least fifteen years."

"Do you think there's a chance it's still safe?"

"It should be."

"What does that mean?"

"It's got cave paintings in it."

"What does that have to do with safety?" His frayed patience showed as he raised his voice.

"The paintings are probably two or so thousand years old," she said, her voice still quietly controlled. "So the cave probably hasn't changed much in fifteen years."

"How would Lexie find this cave?" It sounded like an accusation, even to himself.

Jake cleared his throat. Must have sounded like one to him, too.

"Her father."

"How did Henry know where to find it?" He kept his tone neutral this time, but the more she talked, the more culpable Maude DeVane seemed in his niece's disappearance.

"I drew a map once. I had just finished a really hard rotation and Henry helped me unwind." Her voice sounded far off, as she remembered. "By the time we had made a dent in a twelve-pack, we were reminiscing and he wanted to know how to find my secret cave, in case he ever got to Montana."

It was strange to think of Maude and Henry doing such normal twenty-something stuff as drinking beer. He admitted how little he actually knew about her and his brother's relationship. *Give her a chance.* Henry's words echoed inside his head. He never had.

"So you think he found it from this map?"

She didn't answer this one.

The ride took only ten minutes more, ten long minutes once the conversation stopped and there was only silent jouncing interrupted by an occasional exasperated sound from Jake as he had to slow down to go around yet another obstacle.

Deep in the ranch now, Jake stopped the truck at the split in the road and they piled out. The deep shade of late afternoon light filtering through the pines made the quest seem ominous before they even got started. Please be there, little girl, Guy said to himself.

Jake grabbed the ranch's pack from the back of the truck.

"It's a good hike from here, we start up this ravine." Maude pointed off to the right. "Over a few ridges. You can't see the trail from here, but it's easy to spot once you're up there. The cave itself is hidden from view even from the trail."

She donned a vest, clipped a flashlight to her belt and handed one to Guy. When she grabbed for the pack she had brought, Guy stayed her hand.

"May I?" He picked up the rescue pack.

Maude relinquished it with a brief glance. She kept one of the water bottles and hung it on her belt beside the flashlight. Then with her satellite phone tucked readily in a vest pocket, she started up a rock-strewn ravine. He scrambled after her and Jake after him.

She stopped once and turned. "Please, don't follow too closely. I don't want to kick rocks in your face." But the look she gave him said she wouldn't mind if he got clobbered by one or two anyway.

They quickly left the pine forest behind for rocky hills. Distant mountains turned purple as the sun sank deeper, leaving the sky big and blue and empty.

To keep away dire thoughts, Guy watched Maude ahead of him. He admired how strong and sure-footed she was on the uneven terrain. If she was following a trail, he couldn't see it ahead or behind.

After they climbed out of the next ravine, Maude led them along a tenuous ridge for a short while and then down toward a shallow, rocky stream. She sped up as she approached the bottom, and with one graceful leap cleared the water, landing safely on the other bank.

The farther they hiked, the more he hoped she was not leading them on a wild-goose chase, wasting time they could have spent looking elsewhere.

Guy found himself repeating a silent mantra for Lexie's safety. If he broke the rhythm, it was only to apologize to his brother for losing his daughter, again.

Maude took them up and then down and then up again. To Guy these hills all looked the same, brown rock and scrubby little plants all in deepening shadows. At one point she stopped and picked up several small stones from the trail and put them in her pocket. To protect her from what, Guy wondered.

At last she led them up a rocky trail, wide and easy compared to the others. He looked for footprints, but the stone under their feet told no tale.

At the next switchback, Maude stopped in the shelter of a gnarled pine and Guy stopped beside her. Jake came slowly up the trail behind them as if giving them space.

"It's just up there, beyond the dead tree." She pointed up a small, deep gully.

He nodded, anxious anticipation building at the thought of finding Lexie soon…and terror that they might not.

Maude ascended quickly up the gorge made deeper and darker by the dimming light, and then climbed up onto the boulders behind the tree.

When she disappeared at the top, he started up.

MAUDE CREPT forward across the small flat area behind the rocks. Memories poured in of giggling little girls in worn jeans and flannel shirts, little girls who sneaked away to a place where imagination could fly and parents would never find them. Desperado's Hideout, huge to little girls and old, discovered by people long ago dead, but who left their markings on the walls and ceiling.

A large slab of fallen rock sheltered the dark opening, as if by some grand design nature had built an awning. The two steps down into the cave had always made Maude feel as though she and Amanda were descending into an ancient alien world.

She closed her eyes and watched scene fragments flash inside her head. A ten-year-old Maude squeezing the ring with the ruby stone in the palm of her hand as she fled outside into the snow. Finding Amanda's bed empty. The snow piled high by the wind and the oak tree split in two. And her sister so pale, so frightened, but not afraid of death.

Maude expelled a held breath.

She took the stones she had gathered from the trail and gently tossed them into the dark, low entrance. They clattered for a moment and then fell silent. *Spirits of the old ones, keep us safe, hide us and make the world leave us alone.* She silently said the prayer she and Amanda had used to cast aside any evil that might await them inside. Odd she should remember anything so trivial, but they had always been safe in the cave.

She listened. Nothing.

"Lexie?"

She heard only the last calls of the birds in the dying daylight and Guy scrambling up the trail behind her.

*Oh, please, Lexie. Be here.* She unclipped the flashlight and switched on the beam. As the ray of white light hit the low cave opening a shower of small objects shot out and struck Maude on the thighs and shins.

She jumped back and the projectiles hit the ground around her with a very subtle smack.

Guy heaved himself up onto the rock platform. "Are you all right?"

"I think I might be amused." She stooped and reached for one of the objects. This one was purple and white. Relief tumbled in as she read *Tootsie Pop* on the wrapper. "Yup. Amused."

"Amused?"

She laughed out loud. "She's here."

His eyes narrowed.

Maude chuckled again, and then handed him the wrapper. He studied it and laughed, too. The sound seemed to rumble through her and then out into the valley where it echoed merriment and relief.

"I bought suckers for her at the hardware store."

Jake appeared beside them.

"I'd like to laugh, too," he drawled, "if the two of you would give me a reason."

They looked at Jake's suspicious expression and laughed some more. Maude picked up several wrappers and handed them to Jake. "These just came flying out of the cave."

Jake drew his brows together. "Lollipop wrappers?"

Guy leaned down and called, "Lexie, come out."

The first thing they saw was the spot of her flashlight followed by the top of her red curls as she bent to exit the cave. When she cleared the opening, she stood and challenged each adult with a glare made to look old and experienced by the failing light of the day.

"Are you all right?" Guy asked.

She looked at her uncle as if he were something she found stuck on the bottom of her shoe. "All you said was I couldn't leave the ranch." Then she elbowed her way past the adults and headed down by herself.

"Lexie, wait," Maude called. "It's too dark to go by yourself."

Lexie didn't answer, but the light spill from her flashlight stayed where it was.

"Take her home," Guy said to Jake. "We'll walk."

The cowboy nodded. "I'll make sure she gets there safely."

Maude stepped forward. "Wait. I can't walk back to the ranch house. I have to be available if I'm needed in town."

Guy reached out and snatched the satellite phone from her vest pocket and handed it to Jake. "If they need her, come back."

"Yes, boss."

Maude was sure Jake was grinning by the time he turned away and hurried after Lexie.

# CHAPTER EIGHT

MAUDE CONFRONTED Guy with her hands on her hips. "What do you think you're doing?"

She had no intention of being left behind with a man who couldn't seem to find anything but fault with her. When she tried to follow Jake and Lexie, Guy stepped into the gap between the boulders, blocking any chance she had to exit the small landing outside the cave.

"Crisis intervention," he said.

"What are you talking about? The crisis is over. Lexie has been found."

"Now that I know Lexie is safe, I want to— Well, let's just say, it might be better if Jake took her back and handed her over to Bessie. I'm sure any discussion between my niece and me will be more productive when I'm not so angry with her and she has gotten a good night's sleep." He stepped up closer to Maude and when she aimed the beam of her flashlight into his face, he halted. "In the meantime, we need to talk."

"I think I've been very patient and you've been, well you've been surly and unpleasant. Now, get out of my way." She held the flashlight up this time as if she might bludgeon him with it, and she might. She hadn't decided yet.

"There are things that have to be settled between you and me, and no one will disturb us or overhear us here."

She flashed her beam around in the darkness. "You've got that right." She let her full sarcasm reflect in her tone. She wanted to yell at him, tell him if he had just left the St. Adelbert valley, there would be nothing to settle.

"The happiness of a little girl may hinge on our being on better terms."

"I— Well—" She let her shoulder slump. "I don't have an argument to use against that logic."

Guy leaned on the boulder, his broad shoulders still blocking the opening to the trail. "My place was the loft of a dilapidated toolshed that smelled like old machine oil and older wood."

"Now, what are you talking about?" When the harsh flashlight beam seemed like too much of a desecration of the falling mountain night, she flicked it off—or maybe she didn't want him doing that *studying her carefully* thing he did so well and so unnervingly.

"This place. You used to come here to get away from them."

"Who?" She knew exactly what he meant.

"Anybody who was bugging you at the time."

"My sister and I used to call it Desperado's Hideout. Mom would have forbidden us to come if she knew, and then later I—" She hadn't spoken about her part in what happened to Amanda since she tried to tell their mother all those years ago.

She ducked down, a hand above her head to protect her from the overhead rock, and went inside the cave. Blind, she cautiously lowered her feet down the two steps and stopped in what was probably the middle of the cave. She heard Guy enter behind her and tried not to stiffen when he touched her in the dark.

He stood, close enough for her to feel the warmth of his body, the softness of his breath in her hair. She thought briefly she might stay here in the darkness forever, safe from the slings and arrows of the outside world.

She flicked on her flashlight and stepped farther into the cave.

The small cavern wasn't as big as she remembered, maybe twelve feet high in the center and fifty feet deep. A slight breeze flowed around her, and the soft floor was as it had been all those years ago, covered with millennia of trampled dirt.

"Where does the breeze come from?" Guy asked.

"There's an opening in the far end. During the day, sunlight shows in. The hole's big enough for a little girl to wiggle in and out and to use as a lookout for outlaws or to watch elk lumber by."

"The desperado?" He reached up to touch the crude depiction of a man with only one eye. The bent creature carried what could be construed as a weapon in one hand.

"Most likely a shaman. A desperado to two young girls."

"Does anyone know about these?" He gestured to several drawings sprawled on the ceiling and the walls.

"No. We wanted to keep the rest of the world out of our special place." Maude bowed her head to hide the sadness.

…and after… The cave had offered solace from dwelling on the night Amanda spent lying unconscious in the snow.

"What is it?" He studied her from the edge of the flashlight's scatter.

"I was just remembering—" Amanda's pleading face. *Don't tell them. Please, don't tell them,* Amanda had said, her lips blue, her face pale. Maude wondered if she could sacrifice her older sister's last wish to clear her own conscience.

She certainly could not tell this man. "Why are you being nice to me again?"

She tried to read his expression, and then she tore her gaze away quickly from his face as memories of another kind flared in her mind. Memories of the fire he lit inside her.

He stepped closer. "You came to help without question or recrimination."

"How could you have expected anything different from me?"

"Where Lexie is concerned, I shouldn't." He stooped and picked up an abandoned lollipop stick. "But if we bicker, she'll be torn between us."

She could tell this was hard for him to say. It shouldn't really matter what Lexie thought of her; he was the child's uncle after all and the responsible person in her life.

He crossed his arms as if waiting for her to start. All right, she would, with the nearest and dearest. "Then let's talk about what Mr. McCormack and his pal said to you at the picnic."

"You left before I could explain." He rubbed his forehead as if trying to erase something.

"Please explain it to me now."

He didn't say anything, but took the rescue pack off his back and loosened the blanket from the bottom. With a quick flick, he opened the blanket and spread it on the soft dirt floor. He motioned for her to sit and when she did, he sat on a low rock beside the blanket. He looked troubled and apologetic and sexy. Lordy.

"They asked me to open a practice in town."

Sexy and seditious. She said nothing.

"I told Mr. McCormack I wasn't practicing medicine at all. He took that as an invitation to make me an offer. He is so bent on finding a—"

She held up a hand. "A real doctor? A man?"

He nodded apologetically. "I walked away. Apparently he took that as an *I'll think about it*."

"Mr. McCormack is a sometimes delusional alcoholic, who makes things up to suit his need. I doubt he'll give up on you so easily." Too sexy. Oh, heaven help her.

"About Lexie," he started.

Apparently they were finished with his practicing or not practicing medicine in St. Adelbert or elsewhere.

He continued, "She needs to have all the adults in her life on the same page. The stuff you brought her—"

She shook her head, biting back a smile, instead of contradicting him. For Lexie, she'd hear him out.

"I can't help it if that offends your sensibilities," he said, sounding testy again.

He started to get up and she put a hand on his knee.

"My sensibilities are safe." She pulled her hand away from the fire.

He held her gaze as he spoke. "Lexie needs for you to not interfere with the rules I set up for her."

This time she gave him a noncommittal look, but inhaled his scent deeply until— Oh, my.

"When you brought—" He paused and in the upward-slanting light she saw understanding register on his face.

He dipped his head and put a hand to his forehead. When he looked up, he was smiling. "You didn't give the makeup to her, did you?"

She shook her head. "I brought her bath salts and scented lotion. I thought she might be able to feel a little more grown up without looking the part."

"And you didn't tell her to arrange to meet that kid."

"I'm afraid I didn't know about that until she came to my house."

"I wanted to think you were the bad person in all this." He pushed the hair off his face with both hands. "It seemed like such an easy solution. Cut you out of the equation and everything would be okay."

The muscles in his strong forearms flexed as he brought his arms down, and she found herself wondering what the rest of him was like. She huffed out a breath. "And now?"

He paused and then he laughed. "Jake's right. I'm a one-holed fife."

"She's twelve." Maude said evenly, trying not to betray her desire for this man. "It's the nature of the beast, I'm afraid."

"But when I asked you before…"

She tilted her head and peered at him sternly.

"All right, when I accused you before, you didn't tell me the truth." His words began to temper the sexy feelings she was enjoying, and that was too bad.

"I told you *a* truth and you believed what you wanted."

"Maybe a good parent should be upset by that, but thank you for standing by her."

He shifted off the rock and onto the blanket. When he relaxed back against the rock, she knew a part of his load had lifted.

"Your turn, Dr. Daley. Tell me about you and Henry." Maude wasn't sure he was going to say anything, but then he began in a low, almost reverent tone.

"I was about Lexie's age when Henry was born. My parents are a dysfunctional pair, so I took care of my younger brother as well as a kid could. From a young age, Henry was out there trying to be noticed. Trying to matter to our parents. The more they ignored him, the harder he tried. He was already so wise by the time I went to college.

"I got home as often as I could, but it wasn't enough. When I was in medical school, he ran away and traveled three hundred miles by himself to see me."

"So Lexie came by it genetically."

He nodded. "When he went on his first extreme adventure trip, he didn't tell me until he got back. He showed up at my door with his arm in a sling. Eventually I came to understand the fear was a way of feeling something. He'd go off on his adventures and come back and have me patch him up." He paused and studied her for a long moment. "Maybe I was jealous when he sought help elsewhere."

"He said you were out of town."

"I got back early." Light played across the flexing muscle in his jaw and she wanted to soothe it.

"God, I loved him." It felt good to finally be able to say that to Henry's brother.

"Well, then I don't have to worry anymore that you were only after his trust fund."

"I refuse to get angry at you for that. I used to. One day it occurred to me that you and I both wanted the same thing, for Henry to be happy and safe. The thing I liked most about him in the beginning was that he thought your behavior the day we met was reprehensible."

"I see the gloves are off." He nodded once. "Were you ever after his money?"

She laughed out loud and shifted on the blanket, the soft earth gave beneath her.

"Henry and I had a lot in common. He felt cast adrift in the world and so did I. His family had little time for him. And mine was so far away." She glanced up at Guy. "We settled two things up front. First, if he kept offering money to me, I'd have to stop hanging out with him. We were friends. We loved each other. And the second thing we settled was that we had no sexual interest in one another. He was so damned cute and I was so much older, although I don't think that would have mattered if there had been a gram of chemistry between us. He called us 'soul buddies.' We used to laugh about it and then we'd go to a movie."

Guy peered at her with nonjudgmental interest and she continued. "Oh wait—his money, I did let him buy my movie tickets and I did share his popcorn. He insisted because otherwise, I was so broke, we never could have gone and he so loved movies."

Guy shifted backward and leaned on his elbows. When movement brought him closer, muddle filled her head and she couldn't think of anything more to say.

She wondered if a deep breath would clear her head. She tried. A bad idea. On the light breeze inside the cave, she could smell the remnants of his soap. He wore no aftershave. She liked that in a man; strong artificial scents covered too many of the tantalizing smells the human body offered. She inhaled again, deeply, and closed her eyes. What would it be like to wake up in the morning to that smell? A warm feeling swelled low in her belly.

"Maude?"

She jerked her head up and her eyes open. "Sorry, just lost in the memories, I guess." The memories she might like to make. "Anyway, when Henry found out about Lexie, I was thrilled for him because he was thrilled to have a daughter. I was sad her mother was dead. It's too bad that's what it took for the grandparents to contact Henry about her…" Maude shrugged. "They had so little time together. Two years. It wasn't fair."

He cleared his throat. She didn't look into his face, but was sure she would see her own sadness reflected there.

After a few moments, he gave a gruff laugh. "I had the hardest time putting Kelly into the equation with you and Henry. Although I thought she was perfect for him. After her parents died Henry was such a rock for her, Lexie adored her…and Kelly didn't need his money."

Maude wrinkled her nose at him. "I was so happy when Henry found true love. Kelly was so like him in all the ways I wasn't. He never could get me to be the daredevil the way he and Kelly were. Except maybe driving too fast."

"You? Drive too fast?" He reached out and ran a finger along her jawline. A tantalizing shiver followed his fingertip.

"See how little you actually know about me. As for Kelly, I was surprised to hear she hadn't gone on Henry's last trip. I wonder if she thinks she could have saved him if she were there."

He sat forward suddenly. The indirect light from the flashlight deepened the color of his hair to black, and the shadows accentuated the planes of his face. She knew the look of anguish when she saw it, and on a man like Guy it tore at her heart.

He took in a breath as if he might say something to her, but changed his mind. He'd lost a dear brother. She could relate to that particular pain.

She sat up and moved on her knees next to him. Then she leaned in and pressed her mouth to his. His arm came around her instantly and he pulled her into his lap.

She put her arms around his neck, and when she somehow kicked the flashlight, the bulb flicked out.

Darkness complete and unrelenting surrounded them. There would be no recovery of sight as their eyes adjusted. Night had fallen and it would be inky dark until they turned a light back on or the sun came up.

She started to move away but he stopped her. He cupped her face in his hands and drew her mouth to his, so she leaned against him seeking as much contact as she could find.

Pushing her hands into his thick hair, she luxuriated in the soft, silky texture and then slid her hands down the rippling muscles of his back. Anatomy had never been so sexy.

He pulled the shirt from her waistband and his hot hand sought flesh under her camisole. She gasped when heat closed over her bare breast and lifted her chin when his mouth left hers and trailed down her neck to seek the valley between her breasts.

She pulled on his shirt until it lifted over his head and then leaned against him. The silken hair of his chest against her breasts had her moving back and forth in a swaying dance.

He grabbed her and pushed her back, but only enough to lift her camisole and to lower his mouth to her eager nipple. Heat flooded deeply into her body and she buried her fingers once again in his hair.

Slowly she became aware of a small, persistent alarm playing inside her head. She ignored it as he moved his mouth to her other breast and her nipple peaked instantly for him.

The alarm again, more clearly this time. How many times had she preached, *protect yourself during sex*. But, oh how good to touch and be touched, his hands pressing her to him, his erection so firm and so promising against her thigh.

His mouth descended on hers again and his tongue pressed for entry and she let him in as she reached out with her own.

The alarm clanged louder.

She pushed back and gasped for air, gratified to hear him do the same, also glad he did not get to see her unease. "Are we safe for this?"

He found her hand and put it to his grin. "I am very thoroughly tested and not nearly as used as you might have been led to believe. And you?"

"I'm safe in all ways. Nothing like a hospital in a big city to make you paranoid."

"I never thought I'd be grateful for that." He put a kiss in her hand and then placed her hand on his shoulder.

A sudden fear shot through her. She was safe in all ways, except her heart. She'd never truly been in love.

What if this man was the one, and what if he didn't think so?

He carefully drew her mouth to his as if he sensed her reticence. When he fit his lips against hers, he undid her jeans and dipped his hand inside. The world burst into flames and they sank down onto the blanket. He pulled her shirt and her camisole off, and a shiver of cool air brushed across her belly. A moment later his mouth left hers and the rest of her clothes were stripped from her.

His hand closed over her bare breast and he squeezed, gently capturing the nipple between his fingers. As his hand teased her, his tongue stroked inside her mouth and the fire flared.

She opened her eyes. There was nothing to see in the darkness, and that left her skin and her nipples more sensitive to his touch. She let her own hands roam over the stubble of today's beard and the taut muscles of his chest.

"Fair's fair, buddy. Strip."

"Yes, ma'am," he said in a good imitation of a cowboy drawl, and then never moving more than a few inches from her in the darkness he did so.

It seemed like only a moment later when he stretched out and set fire to her whole body with his hot naked one.

"This is good," Maude said as she exhaled a sigh.

"Let's make it better."

The heat of his mouth closed over her nipple again and when she arched up, he smoothed his other hand down her belly and sank it between her legs.

Oh, she had no idea a fire could burn so madly.

She moved over his body, found his erection with her hand and slowly lowered herself until he filled her.

Together they found a rhythm that allowed them to move among the spirits of the ancient and traveled the path to the welcome, screamingly wonderful oblivion.

Maude collapsed against Guy's damp body and smiled for herself. If this was all there was, if her heart got broken tomorrow, she would not have changed a thing.

After a while, when she started to shiver, he covered her with his body and warmed her again until they were exhausted.

Later, Maude was not sure she could walk across the

cave, let alone back down to the road. She fumbled in the dark and opened the rescue pack to get the spare flashlight.

The light of the small beam rent the darkness and she squeezed her eyes closed, but not before catching a glimpse of him sitting, taut skin over firm muscles put together in a magnificent package.

"Wow." She blinked several times to adjust to the light. "That light is bright."

"Oh, I thought you might be wowing about me," he said and rubbed a finger down her cheek.

"I—um—might have been. We're naked." She laughed. "It was hard to feel naked in the darkness."

"I thought you felt naked and I liked it."

"Me, too."

She reached out and ran her fingers down his chest, luxuriating in the sight and feel of him.

He caught her fingers and kissed them.

Maude examined the cave. "I suppose we can't stay here forever. I don't think Lexie left any lollipops."

"I might risk starvation for this." He brushed a light touch on the inside of her thigh.

"Oh, please, don't do that. They'll find us in a hundred years and won't know what to make of us."

He grinned and handed her a pair of tiny blue panties.

GUY FOLLOWED MAUDE in the dark night. The moon hadn't risen yet, and the beams of their flashlights were all that showed them the way. They had spoken in the cave about much that was between them. She had not told him everything tonight. He remembered the pain in her eyes when he had tried to give her the ruby ring. She hadn't told him why Henry had bought her parents' ranch, and it surprised him to realize he didn't care.

The hike down went without incident and when they got to the clearing by the bridge, Guy found himself chuckling at the sight of Maude's car.

Beside him she gasped.

"So," he asked, "what do you suppose they thought we were doing up here in the cave for so long that we might be too tired to walk to the ranch house?"

"Talking."

He shined the flashlight beam in her face and she snapped her eyes shut, and then slowly opened them and gave him an innocent expression.

When his lips closed over hers, she kissed him back until he stopped and laughed, and then he remembered wondering if he'd ever feel like laughing again. Tonight, in spite of everything, he did.

"I have been so wrong about so many things, Dr. DeVane."

She put her head on his chest, as if she were telling him she had feelings for him, even though they were no longer in the safety of the cave. She forgave him. He tightened his arms around her.

She spoke softly. "I've been wrong about a few things, too."

THE NEXT DAY started with a phone call from Guy that intensified Maude's longing for another interlude in the cave.

The rest of the day went slowly. The patients were a mix of doubtful skeptics and warm welcomers. The people of the town were so polarized, Maude could see Mr. McCormack out there spreading derision wherever he could.

Hopefully her good job and goodwill was spreading faster.

That evening, Maude sat across the table from her parents in her own kitchen. She scraped the last bit of gravy from her plate and looked to see her father doing the same.

She wanted nothing more than to be alone in her room to think about what had happened last night with Guy. It had seemed so shocking in the daylight, but now that the mountains had brought on the shadows of twilight, she found herself thinking about him, wanting him.

"Thanks for dinner, Mom. It was the best meal I can remember in a long time."

Her father looked up and nodded in agreement.

"You should make meals like this for yourself, like… Well, you should." Her mother didn't say it…*like Amanda would do, if she were out living on her own.*

"I manage somehow. Have you seen Amanda recently?"

"Amanda doesn't know who we are." Her mother spoke in a stiff voice, as if she had to force the words out. "She just sits there with that silly smile as if she is amused by the world."

Her mother got up and put her dirty dishes on the counter.

"Mom, I—"

"I wish you wouldn't bring up your sister. You know it hurts me when you do. We go to see her when they call us for something important."

Guilt shot Maude full of gaping holes. She had not been to see Amanda since she returned to St. Adelbert. Her mother might be correct to think Amanda didn't know, but Maude knew. She had blamed her parents for abandoning Amanda, but she had done the same.

"Does she have to be so far away?"

"Great Falls is the best place for her."

"I wanted the best place for her to be here, in town." She said the words almost to herself.

"You know how I feel about that." Her mother's words snapped with anger.

"I'm not a child anymore. Having Amanda near will not send me into daily depressions. It never did."

"I was just trying to protect you."

"I'm sure you were." *I don't want you to talk about that ever again.* How much harm and hurt did protection have to cause? She thought of her mother and herself, of Guy and Lexie.

Then, quickly, she wasn't thinking of Guy's relationship with his niece. She was thinking of a blanket in the cave and she hoped she wasn't blushing.

"What's the matter, dear?"

All right, she was blushing. A lot. "I'm just warm."

Her father got up from the table. "I'm going to do the dishes tonight," he announced.

"And I'm going to get the new samples ready for you to look at later, Maude dear." Her mother swept from the kitchen.

Her father rolled his eyes.

"I can do the dishes later, Dad."

He flicked the small television on the counter on. "No. I'll do them. I'm thinking these dishes may take a couple of hours away from your mother's samples."

"Well, it works for me. I need to go to the clinic. I've piles of things to do."

"And no samples." Her father winked at her and dipped a plate into some soapy water.

Maude kissed him on the cheek. "I'll be back later."

At the clinic she browsed through a pile of dusty old charts. Then she put her elbows on her knees and her chin on her palms. It didn't take long to lose herself in a dark, magic cave. Guy's tenderness. The way she felt when he listened to her and then when they made love. The blissful dark, making everything more sensual, more tantalizing, more explosive.

She clicked her tongue. This wasn't getting many charts triaged. She went over to the file and grabbed another stack.

The sound of the doors opening stopped her. Someone must have seen her car parked out front and came in for help. When she stepped out the office door, a man walked toward her in the dim hallway.

She stopped short. "Hello, Mr. McCormack."

Only the emergency light shone at the end of the corridor, so it was difficult to assess his condition.

"I just thought you ought to know."

"Know what, Mr. McCormack?" She leaned against the wall.

He stopped a few feet away from her.

"Your plan to keep Dr. Daley from practicing medicine in the valley is about to blow up in your face." He spoke with a mild slur. How drunk was he?

"Dr. Daley doesn't consult me as to where he intends to practice medicine."

He lurched closer, and she brought the stack of charts to her chest and hugged them.

"The town council has found someone to replace Doc Avery. If you let Daley practice here, you could maybe stay around to help him."

"Why are you doing this?"

McCormack sneered. "I don't have to explain anything."

"You mean you don't have to explain anything to a woman? I wonder. Would you have the same reaction if I were a man?"

He raised his hand and she steeled herself against flinching.

"Stop." She gave the order firmly as if giving a stat med order to one of the nurses, a command that must be obeyed.

He lowered his arm, but stepped even closer. "Do you really think you can stop me from doing anything?"

"You will be crossing a line if you hit me or anyone else for that matter, and it will be an act you cannot take back."

"You think I'm out of control? You think I can't make rational decisions?"

"I think you need to leave. Go to Missoula or Kalispell. Doc Avery gave you a list of treatment places."

"You'd like that, wouldn't you?"

*Yes, I'd appreciate if it you left me alone.* "No, I'd like to see you happy with your lovely wife and those two great kids of yours."

"You're a joke, Maudie DeVane."

"Is there anything I can help you with, Mr. McCormack?"

"Yes. We'll have a replacement for you soon. We'd appreciate it if you'd go away quietly. We'll arrange the new doctor to take over the purchase of the clinic from you, so there's nothing to keep you."

"It's very presumptuous of you to think I want to turn the clinic over to anyone."

He shot her a hatred-filled look. "Like I said, you can stay, of course. I was just trying to spare you the humiliation of sitting in your office all day with nothing to do. But when the costs have drained all your cash, and you crawl away—"

"You can leave now, Mr. McCormack." She stepped around him and went into her office.

"Oh," he called after her, "Arlene says to tell you she'll continue to do any office work you have for her until the new doctor is ready to start."

His evil laughter faded into the night as he shuffled away and then stopped altogether as the doors closed behind him.

Maude stood in the middle of her office, clutching the stack of charts, shaking with anger and relief. She would not always be able to keep him from violence. He'd grown up that way, she recalled. She felt sorry for him and for his family.

Just as she put the charts on the counter, the clinic doors opened again. She snatched the phone from her pocket. She was not facing McCormack twice in one night.

"Maude. Maude, are you all right," Sally called.

"Sally. Oh, Sally. I'm so glad it's you." Maude rushed out into hallway. "I'm, oh—" Behind Sally, Guy entered the clinic.

Sally looked around and turned back quickly. The faces she made could only be interpreted as, *what's going on,* and then, *ooh la la.* Maude wanted so badly to make a face back at Sally, but she focused on Guy and all she could think of was making slow love in a dark cave.

Sally grabbed Maude's hand and gave a tug to get her attention. Sally turned and they both looked at Guy.

Oh, manners. Yes. "Sally Sanderson, this is Guy Daley."

The two shook hands and Sally gave Maude a narrow-eyed look. Maude thought of what Sally had said of Guy. *Just give me ten minutes with the man*. Maude smiled at the thought.

"Why are you two here?" She looked first at Sally.

"I saw McCormack's car in the lot and yours. I would have been here sooner, but I had a car full of kids and my mom. What did he want?"

"The usual. To tell me to get out of town."

"What did you say?" Guy asked as he stepped forward.

Two days ago, she would have told Guy Daley to go to hell and take that question with him. "I told him I wasn't going anywhere. Now, anyone for ice cream?" Maude looked directly at Guy and smiled. "I'm buying."

## CHAPTER NINE

MAUDE SAT between Sally and Guy on the old wooden picnic table at the ice-cream stand and licked ice cream from a cone.

Sally answered Guy's polite query about being the mother of five, to which he said his previous job might have been easier.

"The jury is still out on the one I'm doing now," he said.

"The executives or Lexie?" Maude ducked to lick the drip racing down the side of her ice cream toward her fingers.

"Seminar leader?" Sally added and guffawed when Guy glared at her for using Cynthia Stone's derogative for him.

"Luckily the executives are gone and the next batch won't arrive until next month," he replied and dipped his tongue down to the cone.

Maude silently admired the way he licked and then willed herself not to explode in a rush of crimson. Sally gave her a questioning look, but like a great friend didn't say anything.

"You never told me what made Lexie bolt the second time," Maude said to Guy.

Guy hesitated and glanced at Sally, who grinned and pointed to herself. "Best friend. You tell her and she tells me or you can tell us both now."

He let out a short burst of laughter. "I took away the rest of the makeup which, by the way Bessie's daughter bought for her. I also took away her phone and forbade her to leave the ranch." He shook his head. "It all worked so well. I expect to be nominated for Uncle of the Year soon."

"How is she now?" Maude knew now how much Lexie's uncle feared for the girl, loved her.

"She's moaning about what a paradise Chicago was."

They licked and then crunched cones until Sally sighed. "Hope you don't have to go to work tonight, Maude," she said. "If you leave, I have to go home and do laundry, or I could go to Alice's by myself for coffee. But then I'd have to hang out behind the canned peas tomorrow to see what's supposed to be wrong with my marriage because I went to Alice's without my family. Small-town life is so interesting. Are you two sure you want to be here? Lexie might be right." She gave them both a Cheshire cat grin.

Maude smiled at Sally to keep from looking at Guy. She wondered what he thought about small-town life, and how long he could manage the scrutiny before he and Lexie flew back to the anonymity of the city. She wasn't sure she wanted to know.

"How long do you think you'll stay in St. Adelbert, Guy?" Sally asked.

Maude groaned to herself.

A siren in the distance brought Maude's head up as she crunched the last of her cone.

"A squad car by the sound of the wail, headed out of town, um, west." Sally looked thoughtful as she said the words Maude had been forming in her own head.

"Sirens mean something different here than they do in Chicago," Maude said to Guy.

"What do you mean?"

"In Chicago a siren means *get the hell out of the way, someone's in trouble*. Here where there aren't so many people, it means your neighbor or a friend is in need of assistance, probably in serious need."

"I never would have thought of it that way." Guy stood, crumpled his napkin and lobbed it into the trash can.

"You would if you stayed here long enough, wouldn't he, Sally." Maude noticed her friend's pensive face. "Sally? What is it?"

"I'm sure it's nothing. My husband and kids are taking my mother home, they'd be out that way." She gave a hesitant point in the direction the squad had gone.

Fear shadowed Sally's eyes, so Maude put an arm around her shoulder and tilted her forehead against her friend's. Guy stood and watched over them like a sentinel. Maude knew the thought of sick or injured people elicited the same feelings of alertness in him as they did in her, no matter how much he protested he didn't want to practice medicine.

After a few minutes passed and Maude's phone didn't ring and there were no more sirens, she let herself relax.

"Guy—" Sally began. Sirens sounded abruptly, filling the night air, followed by the blast of a fire truck's horn, and then they all faded off in the same direction as the squad car had gone.

Maude stood and slid the phone from her pocket and waited for it to ring. A moment later, it did. "This is Dr. DeVane."

She walked away for privacy.

"Dr. DeVane, there's been a car accident out on the highway west of town," a sheriff's deputy told her.

When Maude turned back, she saw Guy sit down next to Sally. Maude silently thanked him.

Every word the deputy spoke brought Maude more on alert and less interested in Sally or Guy. People were hurt, many of them—and some of them were children. She took another step away from Sally and Guy.

The deputy's semicoherent report said things like minivan full of people and pickup and broadside. Eight or nine people, he thought. One was already dead. Between reports to Maude he called out orders and answered questions.

"Do you need me at the scene?" Maude asked.

"It'd be best if you and your team met us at the clinic. There are at least three seriously injured and we'll have them to you in fifteen minutes."

"We'll be ready."

"They're bad, Dr. DeVane, three and maybe four of them. The evac helicopters have already been called. Dr. DeVane?" The deputy paused for an excruciatingly long time. "The van belonged to the Sanderson family."

A horrible, wrenching dread stole her calm. "Who—"

She could hear someone shout at the deputy. "I gotta go," he said in a strangled voice. "It's bad."

—is already dead.

She wanted to scream at her silent phone, but instead she whispered, "Hurry." She closed her eyes in an attempt to rescue her composure before she turned around.

"Maude?" Sally said from right behind her.

Maude faced her friend. "I have to get to the clinic."

Sally grabbed Maude's arms. "It's them, isn't it? It's Peter and the kids. Are they alive? Maudie, tell me, please."

Maude gathered Sally to her. One was already dead, the

deputy had said. Who? "The deputy didn't have many details, but they'll be at the clinic soon."

Over Sally's shoulder, she said to Guy. "You have to come."

"I'll let Bessie know I won't be home for a while," he promised.

By the time the three of them arrived at the clinic, the two nurses and two techs Maude had called raced up the ramp. Each of the four hugged Sally and offered their support and encouragement.

"Sally, they should be here very soon." Maude hugged Sally again. "I don't want to send you into the waiting room by yourself, so you can wait out here near the entrance."

Maude hurried the staff down the hallway toward the treatment rooms where she huddled them and thanked them for coming so quickly. She introduced Guy and gave a brief rundown of his credentials.

"You're that Dr. Daley?" asked Abby, clad in flowered scrubs tonight.

"I suppose I am," he answered, friendly and crisp—professional.

Abby responded with two thumbs up. "Glad you're here."

"We need to count on eight or nine injured, three or four seriously." Maude looked into the faces of her crew. "Abby, call the sheriff's office and check the progress of the evac helicopters. Phyllis, you and Bert set up the main trauma room for two patients, the minor procedures room for the third and the hallway between the two rooms for the fourth. Keep the less injured in the waiting room. Carolyn, get Arlene in here to do the paperwork, and when the deputies get here, see that they keep unnecessary people out."

Maude paused for questions. When no one spoke up, she continued, "You've practiced hard for this. Let's do it."

The lights came up and Maude showed Guy where he could change into scrubs. Five minutes later, when all was prepared, they reassembled.

"The deputy called." Abby spoke up. "He said one of the men from the pickup died at the scene. Nine are on their way and should almost be here."

Sally stood shrinking against the door frame, arms clutched across her chest. Maude went to her friend and wrapped her arms around her.

"They're all alive?" Tears streamed down Sally's cheeks.

"Everyone in your family is alive." Maude hugged harder. "We'll do everything possible to keep them that way. I have to go now."

"There will be two injured in each ambulance," Maude said when she returned to the huddled team. "Dr. Daley and Abby, you take one ambulance. Phyllis, you and I will take the other. Carolyn and Bert, you take the rest and report as soon as you triage them. The EMTs will help when they can."

The doors opened and Maude's mother entered, followed closely by her father. Maude stepped away from her team. "Mother, you shouldn't be here."

"We heard all the sirens. Just give us something to do," her mother pleaded.

Maude exchanged a look with her mother. Both women knew the pain of helpless waiting.

When sirens sounded in the distance, Maude looked over at her friend waiting the vigil of terror. "Mom, you and Dad stay with Sally. She'll need help with her kids when they get here."

"You can count on me, dear." Blanche and Ben DeVane hurried over to where Sally stood.

Doctors, nurses and techs rushed out onto the ramp. A few seconds later, the ambulances screamed up the street followed by the squads. When the vehicles stopped in a line at the door, the rescue-team members flew out of their vehicles and tore open the rear doors.

Maude's heart nearly stopped as a headband with one star broken off fell from the open ambulance door and onto the ground at her feet. "Lizzy," she whispered.

"Five-year-old female, head laceration, nonresponsive when we found her. Thirty-six-year-old male, complaining of head, neck and shoulder pain," the EMT reported as he and his partner worked quickly, unerringly, to get the patients out of the rig.

"How's Lizzy?" Peter's voice came out hoarse.

"Peter, I'm checking her out now." Maude noted Lizzy's breathing and pulse and said a silent thanks for them both.

Strapped to a small backboard, Lizzy looked tiny, her blond hair stuck to her face with blood. The large bandage on her head stemmed further flow.

As the EMTs wheeled Peter and Lizzy inside, Sally rushed forward, followed by Maude's parents. "Peter. Lizzy." Sally grabbed her husband's bloody hand.

"Honey, the other kids," Peter rasped in a desperate tone.

"I'll find them, sweetheart." Sally kissed his forehead.

Sally looked up at Maude with pleading in her pale face.

"I'll let you know what I can."

One of Sally's twins shrieked from somewhere outside and Sally flew out the door, Maude's parents trailing behind.

Maude turned to the work she had to do. "Phyllis, I want these two in the trauma room."

"What happened?" Phyllis asked the EMT as they wheeled the patients inside.

"Pickup ran a stop sign and broadsided the van. Van rolled. This little girl was in her booster behind her father. The truck impacted square on these two."

Maude began a thorough exam on Lizzy.

"Dr. DeVane." Phyllis was holding Peter's cervical collar aside exposing a livid bruise on the side of his neck. Phyllis knew, as Maude did, too much swelling would soon make it impossible for him to breathe.

"As soon as Carolyn is available, we'll get some X-rays," Maude instructed.

She already knew the head wound might not be the worst of Lizzy's injuries. A deep purple bruising of the skin overlay her liver. Internal bleeding could kill her quickly.

The race was on to save man and child.

"Clear." The word snapped Maude's head up in time to see Guy administer a jolt of electricity to Sally's mom. "Sinus rhythm," she heard him say shortly afterward, referring to the return of Mrs. Holloway's heart rhythm to normal.

God, she hoped he was as good as they all said he was.

Abby and an EMT helped a bleeding man with his arm in an air splint onto a cart in the hallway trauma area.

Right now, her job was Lizzy. Maude removed the bandage from the child's head and examined the wound. No overt fracture at the site. *How badly are you injured, little one?* Maude thought.

"Peter. Peter, can you hear me?" Phyllis's voice rose with tension.

"Lizzy," he rasped.

"We're looking after Lizzy, Mr. Sanderson," Phyllis reassured him.

But Maude wasn't certain her words fell on a conscious mind.

"He's out, Dr. DeVane."

"How's his airway and his oxygen level?"

"Holding."

"Speed his IVs up. He might need some fluid."

The two heart monitors offered a steady beep of hope. Children cried in the distance and muffled voices offered comfort. Godspeed, Maude implored the evac teams on the way to St. Adelbert.

Bert and Carolyn came to Maude and reported the others had only minor injuries. The children were all with Sally in the waiting room. Sally had been given instructions to send for help right away if anything seemed wrong. The driver of the pickup would need a few stitches in his hand and he was waiting outside with the police.

"Bert, see if Dr. Daley and Abby need anything. Carolyn, I need abdominal and c-spine X-rays of both these patients, c-spine first on Mr. Sanderson, abdominal second on Lizzy."

The bruise on Peter's neck concerned Maude most, but the steady rise in Lizzy's heart rate and the continued swell of the child's abdomen worried her greatly.

"Come on, Lizzy. Stay with me." If things continued as they were, the child's life could slip away before evac arrived.

"Bill," Maude said to the EMT at her elbow, "see if Dr. Daley can come in here."

A moment later, Guy was at her side.

"Unconscious. Head injury," Maude stated, "but she's bleeding internally. The chopper's not going to make it in time."

He gently palpated Lizzy's abdomen.

"She'd probably die onboard even if it came now." He took Lizzy's hand and turned to Maude. "You have two choices."

"Dire and grim. I know. I need to open her up. I guess I was just looking for confirmation."

He still held Lizzy's little hand in his. "I'll assist."

"Phyllis, get Peter out of here and send Abby in. Carolyn, open an abdominal surgical pack. Bill, get Lizzy's mother in here, please."

"Can you type blood here?" Guy asked.

"Yes, but Sally is compatible. She and her husband took the precaution to have emergency blood sources set up for the children. Sally and Peter carry cards with the information. Between the parents and grandparents, all of the children have emergency donors. Sally's will be enough to get us started."

An eerie calm, of knowing what she had to do and committing to carrying it through to the end, flowed through Maude. People scurried around her and Dr. Daley as they prepped the child for surgery.

Abby set up anesthesia equipment and put it on standby. Guy smiled at her. "You are multitalented."

"You have no idea." Abby grinned appreciative dimples at him and went back to work.

After several precious minutes, a stoic Sally, semirecumbent on a cart in the same room, gave lifesaving blood for her daughter.

Maude held the knife in a steady hand. She glanced at

Guy who nodded his readiness to assist, and then she proceeded. The amount of blood in the surgical field should have frightened her, but she didn't have time for that kind of distraction.

"Dr. DeVane," Phyllis called from the doorway. "I need a doctor right now."

Maude nodded at Guy who stepped away and disappeared through the door followed by one of the EMTs.

"Put sterile gloves on," Maude said to the other EMT. "I need you to help me keep the field clear."

A helicopter whooped onto the landing pad behind the clinic. They would evac the first patient ready and able to go.

"The second and third choppers are hot on his tail," Abby announced when Maude looked up.

"Have them take Peter, Lizzy's not ready to go." Maude bent closer to her work as Abby disappeared through the door.

A minute later Abby returned. "I had to send Mrs. Holloway…she's stable. Peter will be soon."

"Thank you," Maude said, keeping her attention on Lizzy. *Please, Peter, don't die.*

It took what seemed like a small eternity to find the main sources of bleeding in Lizzy's liver and another to pack the spots that continued to ooze blood. By the time the second helicopter landed, Maude had packed the surgical site and Lizzy had a chance at life, because damn it, she was a great doctor. She grinned beneath the surgical mask.

"Lizzy's bleeding is under control," Maude said as she stripped off her bloody gloves. "Sally, we took over a pint of blood from you. Drink the juice Abby has there for you and stay on the cart for now."

Sally gripped her hand. "Please go check on Peter."

"Call if Lizzy changes at all," Maude told Abby.

The hallway appeared as if a bomb had gone off in a medical supply depot. Maude entered the treatment room where Peter Sanderson looked peaceful, but a temporary airway had been surgically inserted into his neck. Maude knew if the swelling didn't subside quickly, they would have to perform a tracheotomy at the next hospital.

"Been busy, have we?" Maude smiled at Guy and Phyllis.

"Nothing out of the ordinary." Phyllis grinned.

"Which one should go first?" This from an evac team member.

"In here." Maude headed toward the trauma room. The evac team followed. When they prepped Lizzy for transport, the child didn't stir.

Maude sent the man with the compound fracture of his arm out in an ambulance. After the last evac team wheeled Peter out the door, Maude and Guy examined the rest of the children and pronounced them officially discharged.

Sally stood beside Maude, tears streaming down her face. "Sally, we'll find someone to drive you to Kalispell."

"I need to take my children. I can't leave them now."

"We'll get you all there." It was Maude's mother. Her dad stood behind his wife looking grim and nodding. "And stay with you as long as you need us."

"But I need safety seats."

"My sister is lending you her kids' seats and her van. It should already be out front." This time it was Abby.

"But I can't take your sister's family transportation," Sally blurted.

"There aren't any *buts*, Mrs. Sanderson." Abby smiled.

"A few of your children's toys, snacks, juice boxes, clothing for you and the kids, diapers, they're all in the van. Mr. Hawes is happy to watch Barney for as long as you need."

"Thank you." Sally hugged Abby and then Maude.

"We'll see you tomorrow or the next day," Ben DeVane said to Maude as Blanche hustled Sally out the door.

Maude watched Abby's sister's van drive away and knew these people were the reasons she wanted to stay here, and after tonight, she didn't see how McCormack and the rest of the naysayers could object to this *woman* doctor.

"I'll sew that one up," Guy said to Maude, referring to the driver of the truck waiting for stitches in his hand.

"No. This one I have to take care of." Maude took the paperwork Arlene had prepared for the man.

"Hello, Mr. Carter," she said as she entered the room, acknowledging the deputy at the man's side. In a community as small as this valley, Maude knew the man might spend a night in jail but would be released in the morning to await his trial and punishment. She wanted so much more for the man who had harmed her friends so grievously.

He stared at her and then at Abby for a silent minute and then bowed his head without speaking.

"Is there anything else bothering you besides your hand?" *Like your conscience?*

He shook his head.

"I'd like to examine you anyway, just to make sure. Abby, would you please get him a gown."

"No." He glared up at her from where he sat on the treatment table.

"It'll only take a few minutes. Just to be sure, Mr. Carter," Abby interjected.

"No. Just sew me up and let me out of here."

Maude did sew him up, quickly and neatly. As soon as Abby applied a bandage and gave him instructions, he bolted with the deputy close behind him.

Maude hated letting a patient involved in a violent accident leave without the benefit of a thorough exam. On TV they held them down. In real life, they had to be let go.

Cleared of patients, debris and staff, the clinic stood eerily quiet. Guy leaned against the door frame of the office, waiting for her to decide if she'd finished enough paperwork.

She looked up. "I have a lovely bottle of white grape juice at home, last year's vintage if I'm not mistaken. I also have beer, if you'd like to come over."

"You put on a good show for the odd out-of-town visitor."

She smiled at him. "Thanks. I hope we did enough."

"If we did more, they'd have to bow to us and burn a calf in our honor."

"Blasphemy."

He laughed and picked up the phone on the desk. "If Lexie's at home, I'll take you up on that beer. If she's not, do you know of any more hiding places around here?"

GUY LEANED on one elbow and pulled the sheet over Maude's beautiful naked body. The ceiling lights blazed and the shade in Maude's bedroom stood open. "You were eager."

She laughed. "I thought I was just responding to your particularly ferocious need."

"Ferocious?"

She nodded. "Delightfully, excitingly ferocious."

"Yeah, I liked it, too." He let his eyes and then his fingers rove over the peaks and valleys of the sheet. "A lot."

As he watched her nipples form little tents in the sheet, he found himself wanting her again.

She smiled as if she knew he had found out her secret and then laughed. "The offer of the beer is still good."

He let his laughter join hers. "We didn't waste any time, did we?" Maude DeVane did that to him. Made him want to feel things again. Made him want to enjoy life. Wonder of wonders.

"You are just what the doctor needed." She leaned over and kissed him on the mouth, letting her tongue linger along the edge of his lip before she pulled away.

"So I'm a mere tool to make you forget?" He feigned sanctimony.

"Hmm. It's all I can do not to say, 'your tool doesn't seem to mind,' but I'd never go there. What I meant was—"

"What you meant was—" He ducked his head under the sheet and kissed her nipple.

"Yeah, that's what I meant."

"Henry said you were sexy." It was odd to think of Henry and not have the thought shrouded in pain.

She pulled the sheet up and gave him a puzzled look. "He did? I didn't know he ever thought about me that way."

"Not for him. For me." It was true; the thought was like an awakening from a dark dream. The many times his brother spoke to him about Maude in glowing terms now came into a different light. "He was trying to steer me toward you."

"You found me." Her voice sounded slightly distracted, but then she tugged him up to kiss her, and he didn't resist sliding his hand down the length of her warm body. "I had heard about post–trauma care sex," she said as she draped lovely limbs over him, "but I've never had it before."

"The information is mostly anecdotal." He pulled her closer and she slid on top of him. "I expect."

"You expect? What? You expect sex after saving lives?" She raised her eyebrows. "You've certainly had opportunities."

He laughed. This was a Maude DeVane he had never allowed himself to know, mischievous and a bit on the naughty side, daring even, to go places most doctors, for all their knowledge about the human body, were reluctant to go. "Most of my post–trauma care opportunities were to treat the next patient and then the next. The rest were to go home and fall into bed."

"And do things like we just did?"

"No, Maude." He touched the tip of her nose with his finger. "But I liked doing the things we just did."

"Maybe we should do them again."

He kissed her in a way he thought should leave no doubt, and then in a long, accelerating stampede of emotion, they took each other over the edge again.

Maude collapsed on top of him and then slid slowly off with one hand trailing on his chest. Even though her breathing quieted, he knew she was not asleep. She didn't feel any more like sleeping than he did. They were exploring something here, something more than sex.

Something new—for both of them he suspected.

"I wonder," she said very quietly.

"What do you wonder?"

She sat up and put on her robe against the chill coming in the window. "I wonder if you're as hungry as I am."

He sat up. "If you're hungry enough to eat a bear, I am."

"Don't have any bear. Don't cook that much, but I've got some mean eggs in the fridge, if you're interested."

With his pants and shirt on, he followed her to the kitchen. Ten minutes later, they were sitting on the window seat where the moon lit their plates of scrambled eggs and toast, and they watched whitetail deer wander in and out of the woods.

"If I could give up something I worked so hard for?" she said without looking at him.

"What?"

"It's what I was really wondering before. Do you miss it? Do you think you'll want to go back to medicine?"

He didn't want to talk about what his life had been before. He didn't want the wound to open up and bleed again.

A small cloud drifted across the moon.

"I don't want you to fix me." The words came out harsher than he expected.

She pulled back and looked at him as if he'd yelled at her. "I wasn't trying to fix you. I was trying to understand. I know how hard I worked to get what I have."

He'd like to say he didn't need fixing anymore, but he knew that wasn't entirely true. Tonight he felt the exhilaration of saving lives again, of working with an experienced team, and he hadn't known how profoundly it would affect him. He wanted it back. He wanted it all back.

But part of it would always be missing.

"Do you know what it's like for your world to go up in flames?" he asked slowly.

She took their dishes and put them on the kitchen table and then sat down on the window seat and pressed against him. When she rubbed his back, he put an arm around her and drew her close. And when she shivered in the cool night air, he pulled her robe closed.

"When Henry died," he spoke even though the words were hard to say, "I thought I could deal with it. I tried to deal with it."

She said nothing. No platitudes. No attempts to cure him of his inability to adjust to his brother's death. No wonder Lexie talked to her. No wonder Henry called her friend for so many years. No wonder Guy felt as if he could be falling in love with her.

"I always felt, I was all Henry had. Our parents never meant to have him and they treated him that way. I was the son. I would be the one to show the world what great people they were. They had no time or inclination to nurture a second child."

She leaned her head on his shoulder and whispered. "Henry and I talked about everything, but he refused to say more than a few words about your parents. In light of what you've just said, so much about Henry is clearer. I miss him."

He felt the loss she experienced, something he had never allowed himself to believe about her.

"It's probably inadequate to say, I wish I'd have given you more of a chance. I'll admit, reluctantly, I was an egotistical sort." He paused, giving her adequate time to absorb and react.

He felt her laugh silently and he put his other arm around her. She had suffered the brunt of that particular personality flaw more than most.

"But after Henry died—" The words faltered, clotted in his brain and he was sure he'd never be able to say them aloud.

She sat silently in his arms, and after a few minutes, he

let her go and the dam broke. "I lost my edge. Hesitated, second-guessed myself. I had to walk away before I made a mistake that cost someone their life. That's when I came here."

"Lexie is lucky to have you."

He let out a gruff laugh. "I have to wonder about that."

"How could anyone love her more than you do?"

"She hates me right now."

Maude smiled. "That might mean you're succeeding."

He leaned down and kissed the lips that knew what he needed to hear, and she reached up and put a soft hand on his cheek. "She misses her father."

"I should have tried to stop him from going to Alaska." Guy turned his head to kiss her palm and then shifted to lean against the wall of the window seat's alcove.

As the dim moonlight slipped softly in the window, Guy hoped the floodgate he had just opened wouldn't let loose a torrent to drown them both.

"Henry loved you fiercely. He understood medicine was your life. It fed you, made you whole." Maude's voice sounded tentative, gentle, as if waiting to understand. "If you had tried to stop him from going to Alaska do you really think you would have succeeded?"

Remembering the face of his rascal brother grinning at him in challenge made Guy smile even as it brought the pain. "I thought I was doing better than trying to stop him."

"What do you mean?" She put a hand on his thigh and stared deeply into his eyes. Her beautiful face showed her concern. Henry had been so right and he so wrong about her. He asked himself, if she knew, would she blame him?

"I was there, in Alaska, with Henry when he died."

# CHAPTER TEN

MAUDE'S EYES WIDENED. "You saw Henry die?"

Guy rubbed a hand over his face trying to decide if he could tell her all of it. Baring the pain made it more real for him and would bring it all up for her to feel again.

Then he realized, since she understood Henry she might understand how he felt.

"We don't have to do this," she said, her voice raw with anguish.

He shook his head. "Kelly backed out of the trip at the last minute. And Henry couldn't figure out why. She wanted to be sure, so she didn't tell him she might be pregnant. It was to have been his coming-home surprise."

She bowed her head in acknowledgment of how horrific that news was.

"Henry told me…" He paused, struggling with whether he had the courage to tell this story at all. When she leaned forward and squeezed his hand, he continued. "He said it was time for me to get off my medical ass and see some of the real world. Said this trip was safe enough—just backpacking and grizzly-bear avoidance. The only real danger was supposed to be getting bored with freeze-dried food. It was summer, after all, in the Brooks Mountain Range."

"Brooks, that's isolated country above the arctic circle, right? That sounds like Henry's version of a safe trip."

He barked a laugh. "Our guide lived there, hiked for business and pleasure and Henry said, *when he's finished with us, the guide's taking out a Cub Scout troop.*"

She smiled at Henry's kind of humor.

"I thought if I went with him, I might get to know him, learn to understand him, and up to a point, I did get to know him better. I knew he was seeking the high he got by going where few ever tread."

Maude squeezed his hand again and he squeezed back to let her know he appreciated her listening to him.

"We were trying to reach a higher camp. It was beautiful. The sky was blue and the clouds kept hiding and then showing off the mountain peaks. The mountains aren't record setters for height, but the amount of wildlife there is amazing, and we had just hiked across a valley of grasses and wildflowers."

She let him roam around in his memories and he was grateful for that.

"We were almost there. All we needed to do was climb up to the top of a ridge. I use *climb* loosely. We weren't roped and using pitons or anything. It was just steep and hard work after a full day's hiking. It was Henry's turn to be the last man up and I was ahead of him.

"The last several yards were tough going. I lost my balance. Henry grabbed for me to keep me from plunging down the steep ridge…and he fell." Guy rubbed the scar at the corner of his eyebrow remembering his desperate scramble to get to his brother.

"I'm so, so sorry. How… I mean, oh my God." She leaned in and put her arms around him.

"I held him in my arms and… I broke every promise I ever made to him. I let them all down." Pain blacked out everything else, but he forced himself to finish. "I couldn't even keep him alive long enough to get him in the rescue helicopter. And no matter how much I rationalize, I cannot make that right."

Black sorrow emptied him.

"Was there anything you could have done?" Maude asked quietly, lighting the void a little.

"How many times I've asked myself that question. No, there isn't, but he's dead because I was there."

The pain in her eyes reflected his pain. She had said her sister lived in Great Falls. She might know how fierce love for a sibling could be, but it was foolish to think telling her could fix this, foolish to think anyone could understand. "Thank you, Maude, for listening. I don't expect it to be easy to understand what it's like to lose a sibling, and to feel responsible."

The sorrow on her face turned to horror.

"I'm sorry to have brought it all back for you." He gently disengaged from her arms. "I'll call you tomorrow." He kissed her on her slightly parted lips, grabbed his shoes and keys and walked out the door.

MAUDE WATCHED GUY leave. One brother she loved was dead and the other brother she now knew she loved blamed himself. *I don't expect it to be easy to understand.* She had to let him walk away thinking that, because the pain she had lived with all these years had threatened to well up and spill out all over his grief.

THE NEXT DAY, Guy sat in his office at the ranch studying the latest job offer from St. Margaret of the Bleeding Heart

Hospital in Chicago. He had thrown it away twice and fished it out from the trash both times.

The sun had come up again today, just as it had yesterday, but once again, nothing in his life was the same. He had thought he could bury himself on a ranch in Montana, but last night working with Maude, having her question whether or not he could live without medicine, had him examining his skewed path.

Lexie seemed unhappier as the days went by, yet she had run here from Chicago.

When the doorbell rang, he found himself hoping it was Maude, but the person who answered Bessie's query was male.

Soon, Bessie appeared in the office doorway. "Dr. Daley, Mr. McCormack would like to talk to you."

*Shoot him.* Guy cleared his throat. Being out in the Wild West must have affected him more than he thought.

"Send him in, Bessie." He turned the job offer facedown on the desk.

McCormack appeared, red hair neatly plastered to his head, dressed in a suit as out of place on him as a tutu would have been on Jake.

"Good morning, Dr. Daley." He approached Guy with his hand extended.

Guy stood and shook hands but stayed behind the desk.

"I hope you don't mind my stopping by," McCormack said in a conciliatory *aw shucks* kind of tone. "I came to ask you to keep working here in the valley. We sure could use you."

"Have you talked to Dr. DeVane today?"

McCormack dismissed the idea with a wave of his hand and took a seat he wasn't offered. "She would have been totally out of her element if you hadn't been there to save those people last night. It would have been a real disaster."

"It was a *real disaster* for a few families in the area."

"It would have been much worse if you hadn't been there." McCormack slouched down into the chair and stretched his legs out. "The talk all over town is you saved those people."

"This valley couldn't have a better doctor than Dr. DeVane." He didn't know why he was defending Maude to this horse's ass, when all he wanted to do was wipe the sneer off the man's face and toss him out the door. How much alcohol had McCormack already had today?

"Well, maybe she could help you out. I'm sure some arrangement could be made to let her stay."

"Mr. McCormack, I have work to do. Goodbye." Guy picked up the deer-in-the-mountains snow globe from the desk and tipped it once to start the snow falling.

"Hmm." McCormack cleared his throat and pushed up from the chair. "I'll check back with you and see how things are going. As long as you're still here, we have a chance."

Grinning like a demented mule, McCormack backed away until he was out the door and closed it behind him. He must have known Guy wanted to bounce the snow globe off his head.

A scant two minutes later, the door popped open and Lexie stomped into the office. She had both her fists clenched and jammed onto her hips.

He smiled. With her scrubbed-clean face, she looked twelve. "Good morning," he said.

"Where were you last night?" She threw herself down on the green leather couch.

Today she wore jeans and a pink sweatshirt she called

a *hoodie*. She looked cute, and she'd clout him if he said so. Instead, he came around and sat on the front of the desk. "There was a car accident and I stayed in town to help Dr. DeVane with the injured people."

"You were a doctor again?" Her eyes lit up.

"Yes, I guess I was."

He watched the wheel in her head turn and the expression on her face change. Lexie saw most things in black and white. Figuring that out had made it seem as if he might actually understand her, a little, someday—maybe, when she wasn't being mercurial.

After thinking for a moment, she threw both hands in the air. "Yippee. That means we can go back to Chicago again. Before school starts."

"I didn't say I was going back to medicine." Very mercurial. "I thought you liked the ranch and the people here."

"It's okay here, but I'd like it better if the ranch was in Chicago." She leaped up from the couch and jumped up and down. "I can see it now." She giggled and he found himself laughing out loud along with her. "Okay. Okay. Can you see Jake riding old Timber up the Magnificent Mile?"

"I can see him tying the horse up at the Old Water Tower."

"I know. I know." She laughed harder. "And I want to see him in a tux and shiny shoes like you and Dad used to wear sometimes."

Jake stepped into the doorway. "Who's going to wear shiny shoes?"

They both burst into guffaws.

"You!" Lexie pointed at Jake as she fled giggling.

Guy looked at Jake. "I suppose you came here for something besides to be laughed at."

Jake turned his cap in his fingertips. "If it will make that little girl laugh like that, I'll wear purple patent leather shoes, boss."

"And a tutu?"

He nodded once. "And a matching tutu."

"Thanks, Jake, I appreciate it."

"I was just about to leave for the hunter's cabin. Needs to be checked, and Bessie's got some supplies to be delivered. Just wanted you to know where I'm going."

"I'll check it, take the stuff. I've never been inside the cabin." And it was Grand Central Station in his office—as well as his mind. A trip to the cabin might be just what he needed.

"Much obliged." Jake handed him a paper with Bessie's precise demands. "Do a good job, boss, 'cause she'll hold me to it."

Guy smiled and scanned the list. "There doesn't seem to be anything on here I can't handle."

Jake nodded. "Supplies are already loaded in the truck."

Guy scanned the list again and when he glanced up, the doorway was empty.

Well, now he had some idea of how Lexie felt about moving to Chicago. If he only knew if he could ever face big-city medicine again. And what about Maude?

"Good morning, Dr. DeVane." Guy heard Jake greet Maude at the front door.

He let the sweet anticipation of seeing her fill him. He hoped she brought good news about last night's patients, but most of all he wanted to touch her, hold her in his arms. Tell her he was sorry he walked away from her last night.

Thoughts of St. Margaret's, of leaving, seemed totally irrelevant.

As she and Jake exchanged pleasantries in the
hallway, Guy rose to lock the packet from St. Margaret's
in the file cabinet.

When he turned, Maude entered the office and by the
disappointment on her face, didn't expect to see him
behind the desk.

"Looking for someone?"

MAUDE SPUN to see Guy smiling at her and all apprehen-
sion she had about coming today fled as a sharp desire
filled her.

"You startled me," she said.

He closed the door and in the same movement, swept
her into his arms. His dark eyes sparkled with desire as his
mouth closed over hers.

"Good morning to you, too," he said when he leaned
back to look at her.

She put both palms flat on his chest and studied his face.
"Are you all right?"

"I am."

"You miss him. That I understand."

He covered her hands with his. "It's easier to be by
myself when I'm like that. Less apologizing and explaining later."

"Explaining and apologizing unnecessary. I came
because I wanted to tell you in person. I got calls this
morning from both hospitals where the evacs took our
patients. Lizzy woke up during the night. She's stable.
They all are."

"Sometimes the magic works," he said as he smiled

and gave her a mischievously sexy look. "Do you have patients today?"

"This afternoon."

"I was just about to go check out the hunter's cabin, make sure it's stocked and in good repair."

She found herself watching his mouth as he spoke, remembering the magic it could do on her body.

"Maude?"

"Oh. Yes. The cabin. Bessie has a list for everything else, does she have a list for the cabin?"

He flourished a piece of paper. "Want to help me?"

She wanted to do many things to him. "I don't feel like...turning you down."

They tried not to run down the hallway and out the front door to the truck, especially since Bessie was already grinning at them.

A few minutes later, they were headed into the sunny wilderness of the back acres of the ranch. Trees, meadows, butterflies, flowers, the stuff of summer. The day seemed brighter than usual. Maude reached over and put her hand on Guy's thigh and he covered her hand with his and smiled.

The elevation rose as they got deeper into the forest, and memories flitted in and out like shadows. Little girls. Grandmother hobbling along with her cane. A lonely teenager.

"Once a year, our parents let us spend the night in the cabin," Maude said to control the gathering memories. "When Amanda was fourteen, Dad and Mom let her and a friend stay. She and I never got back there together. Things interfered."

"Things have a way of doing that." He smiled at her again. "I've only seen the place from the outside."

She laughed. "Then you've seen most of it. It's very austere inside. Or it was two decades ago when I last saw it."

"So no satellite TV or video games?"

"No mattresses, only platforms, a few sticks of furniture, and a few rudimentary supplies. Not exactly the Ritz. Dr. Avery used it once in a while. Called it his remote vacation spot."

"What was Dr. Avery like?"

"My sister thought the sun rose and set with him. From the first day she helped out at his clinic, she dreamed of taking over his practice and of being the valley's doctor one day. Strange how things work out."

"Strange?" He brushed a finger down Maude's cheek and she leaned in, eager for more of his touch.

"Amanda's dream is the reason I'm in medicine. When she couldn't do it, I sort of took over and now I'm living her dream."

He stomped on the brake, jerking them in their seat belts, and stopping the truck in a cloud of dust.

"What's wrong?" Maude looked around for a stray animal or fallen tree, the usual reason for sudden stops on this old road.

He stared at her with a puzzled look on his face. If he'd have sprouted horns, she couldn't have been more surprised.

"What?" she finally asked.

"Your sister's dream? You're living your sister's dream?"

"What's wrong with that?" Why was he so shocked?

"Somebody else's dream may have been the reason you went to the first day of medical school." He made a scoffing noise that she did not appreciate. "But I've seen you at work. After that first day, the dream was all yours. No doctor as good as you are gives that much for someone else's dream."

He turned away and started driving again.

She wanted to argue, but found she couldn't.

"I hate it when other people can see inside my head when I can't." This time she swatted at him when he reached out to touch her.

He laughed and put both hands on the steering wheel. Around the next bend in the road, the cabin came into view.

When he stopped the truck this time, he leaned over and pulled her close, kissing her mouth. The desire smoldering in her burst into flame, and she opened her mouth and sought more. A few minutes of luxuriating in the feel of his kiss, of his roving hands, and she pulled away. "Oh, wow. I would have thought I was beyond making out in a car."

He gave her an amused look. "Truck."

"Making out in a truck then."

"Don't mind if I do." He kissed her again.

When she found herself wanting him right there on the seat, she stopped and laughed. "I'm not doing it in a truck. Besides, didn't we come here to do a job?" She pressed her lips to the dip at the base of his throat and inhaled the smell of him as she did.

He pushed her away by both shoulders. "If you don't want to do it in a truck, then don't do that in a truck."

She tried to lean in again, but he held her at bay and gave her a mock stern expression. "We're getting out…of the truck…now."

He opened his door and hauled her out after him. He kissed her once, hard, and then went to get the clean blankets and supplies from the bed of the pickup.

She could not resist, and pressed her hands to the seat of his jeans and squeezed.

He made a growling sound deep in his throat.

She laughed. "I'd forgotten how much I like the sounds of nature."

When he spun around with the armload of stuff, she sprinted away toward the cabin.

The cabin appeared as it had two decades ago, sturdy timber construction, shuttered windows. Only the wooden bench under the overhang, added by her father when she was a small child, showed the passage of time.

She pushed open the door and stood on the threshold. The air inside smelled of must and old smoke. The two barren platforms, a fireplace and the rough-hewn table with two chairs looked exactly as she remembered. A kerosene lamp still hung from the ceiling, and a rodent-proof cabinet sat in the far corner, another of her father's additions.

Maude stayed in the doorway. "Wow, I could be ten again," she said, smiling because the paralyzing feelings she expected to have didn't materialize.

Guy nudged her inside with the pile of blankets he held in his arms. "If you were ten, then the things I'm thinking would be against the law."

"Hmm. Then I'm glad I'm not." Maude crossed the room and opened the metal storage cabinet. She grabbed blankets and such stacked inside and dumped them on one of the wooden sleeping platforms.

"Let some fresh air in" was on Bessie's list, so she

opened both windows. Maude stayed at the second one and leaned her elbows on the sill. Crisp mountain air washed over her and made the early wildflowers outside sway.

"Do you suppose these blankets ever get used?" Guy asked.

"Sometimes," she said as she gazed out at the swaying of the summer grasses surrounding the cabin. "I don't know when or if these blankets were used."

"What's this?"

Maude turned from the window to see Guy holding up a small framed drawing. She knew the sketch from a long time ago. It was a woman and her daughter. The ring, its stone accentuated on the drawing by a red splotch, the color of blood, seemed to reach across time and accuse her. Two decades of pain slammed into her. The rush of emotion froze her into a pillar of ice threatening to shatter

GUY WATCHED as Maude froze. The stricken look on her face had him at her side in three quick steps. She tried to move away, but he held her close.

"Mother's Most Precious Possession," she said in the smallest voice.

Guy turned the drawing over and the words Maude had just spoken were scrawled across the back. He looked at the picture again. The pencil drawing was quite good. Two women. The younger woman obviously adored the older one. There was one spot of color in the drawing. The older woman had a ring on her finger and its stone had been penciled in red. "Maude—"

She stood, stiff, staring at the drawing. Horror etched on her face.

"The ring I tried to give you?" he asked.

She nodded. He put the drawing facedown on the table. Then he took her arm and led her to the bunks where she had dropped the items to be taken away. She sat without a fight.

"Do you want to tell me about it?"

She moved back to lean against the wall propped up on the bunk. Moisture collected in her eyes, but no tears fell. "I thought the drawing had been destroyed. Dad must have stored it here. He's always been so stoic, I sometimes wondered if he felt anything. I guess he did."

She stayed quiet for several minutes. He knew well the war that must be going on inside her head. To tell or not to tell. "I told you mine. Now you tell me yours."

"It seems so self-indulgent, so—so—"

"Icky?" The world was filled with icky according to Lexie. He prodded the toe of Maude's shoe with his, and she responded with a grim smile.

"It was worse than icky," she said in a quiet voice.

He sat down beside her, and to make her more comfortable he swung her feet up and then his. Their shoes clunked on the bare wood of the bunk.

"That's my mother and my grandmother in the drawing. Amanda drew it when she was ten or eleven."

"She's quite talented."

"She was."

He wondered at that, but decided to let the tale unfold as it would.

"When Grandmother died, our mother cried for so long, Amanda and I thought she might die of a broken heart. It was pretty frightening for a couple of young girls. Grandmother left the ring to Mother who called it her most precious possession and forbade us to touch it."

He moved back to lean against the wall beside her, and she put her head on his shoulder. The smell of her seductive scent filled his head.

"When I was ten, Mom and Dad left Amanda and I home alone and Amanda was put in charge, as always. This time I got very petulant about it. I guess I wanted to do something that showed them all that I couldn't be controlled. I went to Mother's room and took the ring from its box."

"Forbidden fruit?"

She nodded. "I took it and I meant to return it, but my parents came home unexpectedly and Mom almost caught me. I panicked and ran outside into the snow. And I…I lost it. It disappeared into the snow and I didn't see it again until you tried to give it to me." Her voice came out in a thin trail of confession.

"That night, I wanted to go out and look for it after our parents went to bed. It was snowing and the wind was blowing and Amanda insisted I go to sleep.

"The next morning, her bed was empty and I found her pinned under a limb of an old oak tree. Her face was so pale—her lips trembled as she tried to talk. 'Don't tell them,' she said. 'Don't tell them you took the ring. They'll know I wasn't a very good big sister.' She was so cold, I put my coat on her, and I tried so hard to move that limb. Then I ran to get help.

"By the time dad cut the branch away, she was barely breathing, and the ride into St. Adelbert's in the truck was long and terrifying. In the clinic, the only thing I remember was someone shouting, 'her heart's not beating,' and then they took me away and I didn't see Amanda for months."

"I thought you said she lived in Great Falls."

"In a nursing home."

*I don't expect you to understand.* Remorse socked Guy in the gut as he remembered his words from last night. "Maude, I don't know what to say. *I'm sorry* seems so useless."

"She was so smart and talented and beautiful. She truly was a golden child, and the best thing about her was that she loved me just the way I was."

Her words made Guy realize being a doctor was not her dream. Her dream was to stop being second best. Henry had bucked that trend for so long, and Guy's love hadn't been enough to save his brother. This valley was where Maude could find the place inside her where she felt whole. And his being here only muddled matters for her.

"Maybe we should go," he said, although leaving was the last thing he wanted to do. "Things are so unsettled, I'm not sure we should—"

She quickly pressed her hands flat on his chest, and looked into his eyes. "I don't care if the whole world falls apart, I think we should stay right here for a while."

He pulled away long enough to fluff the blankets and pillows into a nest, and then he took her into his arms.

His world might go up in flames again at any moment, but this time, for a little while, he wouldn't care.

THEY ARRIVED BACK at the ranch house to find Lexie pacing the deck outside the front door with a fistful of papers in one hand. When she saw the truck she flailed her arms in the air and shouted something Guy couldn't understand.

She did not look happy.

As soon as the truck stopped, Lexie ran up and slapped a hand down on the hood with a loud thud. "How could you? How could you?"

She shook the papers at him with both hands.

He leaned out of the truck window. "Lexie? I'm going to park in the shed and then I'm going to say goodbye to Maude. When I'm finished, I'll be in the house to talk to you."

She made a rude sound and looked petulant and sad at the same time. Emergency medicine was easier, without a doubt.

"What's she got?" Maude asked when Lexie had gone back up onto the porch.

"I'm not sure, and I hope I live to find out."

Maude gave him a gentle and understanding smile. "I'd stay and try to save your life, but duty calls."

He pulled the truck into the barn out of sight of the house. When Maude got out, he kissed her well and good, as if it might be the last time.


GUY FOUND LEXIE perched on the arm of the sofa when he got to the office. Eyes closed, legs and hands moving, she was deeply tuned into whatever was playing loudly through the headphones, but her hearing was an issue for another day.

From the doorway, he spotted a creased and crumpled stack of papers on his desk. He recognized the offending documents immediately. They had arrived a few days ago, the newest batch from his parents' attorneys. They were suing Kelly for custody of Lexie and for the ranch. Guy knew they didn't really want the child, but they would have a list of altruistic reasons for trying to control as much of Lexie's world as possible.

As he walked past her, Lexie flew off the couch and snatched away the stack of papers.

She yanked the headphones from her ears as she circled him. "What is this? What's going on? You don't tell me anything. Are you sending me away? When were you going to tell me?"

Pain and anger radiated from her, tears flooded her eyes and she crumpled onto the couch. "I wish my mom was still alive."

"Do you know what the expression *blowing smoke* means?"

She glared at him.

"That means your grandparents, my parents, are having their attorney throw these papers at us in the hopes we'll think they mean something legitimate, something real."

"I won't go live with them. I'd rather be a street person."

"They don't have a chance of getting custody of you away from Kelly. I'm going to be honest with you. What they want is the ranch."

"The ranch? You people are all fighting over my ranch? Well, they can have it, but they can't have me. I won't go live with them. The last time they sent me to that school and I had to wear a uniform and share a room with three other girls and they left me with the cook when they went on a trip."

"Your dad was furious when they did that. That's when he decided you were better off living with him, a single dad, than with your grandparents. And that's why he left Kelly as your legal guardian instead of your grandparents."

She grabbed the pillow beside her and hugged it close. "My mother said my dad didn't want me. How could she say that when he didn't even know about me? He said he loved me, but did he love me?"

Guy sat on the edge of the desk to face her as he struggled to place her questions into a linear context so he could understand and answer them.

"I didn't know your mother. They weren't quite sixteen when you were born."

"Kids for parents. That's kind of icky."

Remember that for a very long time, he thought. "Lexie, I'm glad you're as smart as you are."

"Now that I'm older, I've been thinking stuff about my life."

"Do you want me to tell you what I can?"

She gave him a sulky look but nodded.

"Your dad didn't know you existed until a few months after your mother died in the car accident. Your mother's parents realized it wasn't fair to keep you from your dad all your life and I think they might have had money problems. That's when they brought you to your grandfather and grandmother Daley for them to assume custody of you."

"I was a little kid," she whispered. "All I knew was my mommy was gone and Grandma and Grandpa didn't want me anymore." A tear started down her cheek. "And my dad didn't love me."

Guy pressed his hands on his thighs and leaned toward her. "He didn't know how. He had never met you and he was in college. He thought it might be best if he left you with someone who knew what to do with a child. At that point, it wasn't a matter of love."

"That's crap."

"Lexie." They had the language discussion often enough, he didn't have to elaborate for her to understand.

"Well, it is."

"That may well be. If I'm going to be honest, it never occurred to me that I could, or should, step in, either. When your mother's parents needed someone else to take you, it seemed Grandma and Grandpa Daley were the best choice." He pressed his hands down his thighs. "But about the papers from your grandparents' attorneys, they mean nothing. So what do you think of the truth so far?"

"I wish I knew him better."

"I can tell you that he was tickled to death that he had a daughter."

The forlorn look on her face tore at his heart.

"I'd hug you now if you let me." He held out his arms. She glared at him.

He shrugged one of her one-shoulder shrugs at her. "I just thought you ought to know. Some of us want to hug you sometimes."

"Yeah? So, what about the other letter?"

# CHAPTER ELEVEN

"OTHER LETTER?" Guy asked. He knew the job offer from St. Margaret's was locked in the filing cabinet, and now he knew the letter from his parents' attorney should have been in there.

Lexie sat on the couch with her arms folded. By the way she looked at him, he'd have to evolve a few million years to elevate himself to the level of pond scum.

"Bessie brought the mail back from town this morning. There was a letter from Kelly and I opened it." She tossed the pillow aside and gave him one of the defiant stares she used when she knew she had done something wrong and *what was he going to do about it.*

He wanted to shake some sense into her. He wanted some bright light to come down from above and tell him what he was supposed to do with a twelve-year-old. He wanted to hug her.

"That's it," he said in his most stern tone. "From now on, I'm reading your diary."

"You can't—" She halted the sanctimonious rant before she got it off to a good start and tried hard not to smile. "I don't have a diary."

He grinned at her.

"If you ever do, I'm reading it until you stop reading

my mail." For now, he was going to have Bessie lock the
incoming mail up safely until he could get to it.

Lexie seemed as if she was considering the value of that,
but her expression quickly changed back to pond scum
mixed with anxiety. "She's trying to give me up. Kelly
wants you to— What did she say? Oh, yeah. She wants you
to take sole custody. That means she doesn't want me
anymore, doesn't it?"

"I thought you didn't want to live with Kelly and the
baby. Have you changed your mind?"

"I didn't. I don't. Oh, I don't know. I liked Chicago.
There's more to do there."

"More places to shop?"

"Yeah." She fiddled with the tab on her sweatshirt for
a bit and then stopped and looked up at him. "Uncle Guy,
I know why Dad didn't love me right away."

"You know?"

"I know because I hate little Adam. I know I'm
supposed to love him because he's my baby brother and
all, but I didn't ask for him and he, well, he takes all Kelly's
time and she didn't have much time for me anyway, since,
since Dad died."

Guy had seen his brother's son a couple of times, but
Kelly had been distracted and very protective. "Did you
think he was cute?"

The corner of her mouth sneaked up. "Sometimes."

"Does he know you don't like him?"

"He's a baby." Her tone implied *you idiot*. "Babies don't
know anything."

"They might."

"I'm always nice to him, 'cause Kelly's always there."

"Do you think you wouldn't be nice, if she wasn't?"

"I thought about it once, but I felt so bad, I asked Kelly to let me rock him to sleep." Lexie stopped wiggling and smiled. "And she let me. She doesn't always let people hold him, especially Grandma and Grandpa Daley."

"What do you think that means?"

"She didn't want me to feel left out?"

"Good guess. Can I see the letter from Kelly now?"

She handed crumpled papers to him. The first page was a note from Kelly. She wanted to relinquish custody to him if he thought that was best. The rest were papers for his signature. When he finished, he focused on Lexie.

She drilled him with a ferocious look, arms folded in challenge. "That leaves just you."

"Just me? Well, gee thanks."

She snorted out a breath and then wiped her nose on her pink sleeve. "What if you decided to give me up? What if you died? Then what would I do? Where would I go?"

He took the tissue box from the desk and tossed it to her. "I wish I could foresee the future."

She sat up on the edge of the couch and blew her nose. "Well, make a guess."

"Lexie, I don't plan to give you up, ever."

"My mom and dad didn't plan to die."

She seemed so intent that he knew his answer must be judicious without seeming patronizing.

"I think it's fair to give you a say in what happens to you." He spoke slowly, so she wouldn't feel she was getting an off-the-cuff answer. She'd probably had too many of those, many from him. "What would you like to happen to you if I died?"

This time she sighed. "I guess I'd go live with Kelly and little Adam if I had my choice. He's not so bad, especially when he's not being icky and puking and all."

"Then I'll make sure that's what happens in the event something happens to me."

She sat quietly, kicking her feet up and down in time to some tune inside her head. "Uncle Guy, what happened in Alaska?" She bit her lower lip and stilled her feet.

When he looked into her clear blue eyes, the eyes of her father, it was as if for the first time, the total ramifications of what had happened in Alaska flooded in to swamp him. Facing Maude had been painful, but with Lexie it could be treacherous.

Henry might have just now died in his arms for how he felt in that instant. He bowed his head. What could he say to her?

"You can tell me. I might be a kid, but I can take it."

He told her, without the grim details, and watched her closely for signs she was getting too much information. He told her about her father's fall, about the descent to try to rescue him, about Henry's dying without even getting a chance to say goodbye.

"I let you down, Lexie. I let you all down." Guy couldn't look into those innocent eyes anymore, so he looked down at the pattern in the parquet floor.

"That's pretty selfish."

He snapped his head up. She had come over to stand in front of him. Red curls surrounded the face of a little angel. She had her own guilt and her own need to be loved. Henry's death didn't all belong to him.

"It is, Lexie. It is pretty selfish of me." And he realized he never quite gave himself permission to feel that way before. Too many years passed where he knew if he wasn't responsible for Henry, no one would be. When Henry became an adult, not much changed.

"But it's okay."

"Really?" he asked.

Sometimes she was so much older than twelve.

"I'm the princess of selfish. Dad was prince. I think we all got it from Grandma and Grandpa Daley." She crawled up onto the wooden desk to kneel beside him and put her arms around his neck, and then tentatively lay her head on his shoulder. "Maybe it's how we try to keep from losing him completely, Uncle Guy, by hanging on to him any way we can."

The words of a child.

He cried then—for the first time since his brother died. And when she joined him with her arms still around his neck, her face pressed into his shoulder, hot tears soaking through his shirt, he knew they might both begin to heal.

MAUDE HAD FINISHED with her last patient as twilight colored the sky. Later in the afternoon things had gotten odd at the clinic. Two patients left before she got a chance to see them. Later ones canceled their appointments altogether. More than once, when she came out of an exam room, the chatter in the lobby quieted instantly. She had thought she was being paranoid.

At any rate, she avoided the grocery store on her way home. The last thing she needed was to hear half truths from behind the toilet-paper display.

Now she was sitting on the window seat in her kitchen, dressed in a fleece warm-up suit and eating a bag of baby carrots. Maybe the forest outside her window could make some sense out of the day.

Thinking of the time she had spent with Guy still left her breathless. She knew she needed to enjoy him while he was here because he'd have to leave. He'd need the challenge big-city medicine gave him and she needed this hopelessly out-of-date little valley.

He had been so right to say practicing medicine was her dream. Practicing in this valley where she had come from would make the dream real.

She was about to bite a carrot in half when someone clomped up the wooden steps outside her kitchen door.

She opened the door to see a grim-looking deputy standing on her porch with his cap in one hand.

"Hello, Deputy." She greeted him with a sense of dread creeping into her.

"Dr. DeVane." The deputy tapped his cap on his pant leg. "It's Shelby Carter."

The name of the driver who had caused the accident with the Sanderson family made the dark dread draw up around her throat.

"Is he coming into the clinic?" She cleared her throat as her brain scrambled for a reason why the deputy would be here to tell her this.

"I'm afraid it's too late."

Maude squared her shoulders and automatically switched into doctor mode. "Tell me what's going on, Deputy."

"He's dead, ma'am."

"Are you sure? Maybe if I…" If only he had let her examine him after the accident.

"No, Doctor, he's gone."

"But…" If she'd been able to change Mr. Carter's mind.

"There might have been something you could have done if they'd have found him earlier, but not now."

"Do you know what he died from?"

"No, but they should almost be at Fuller's Funeral Home by now. Do you want me to divert them to the clinic?"

The deputy tried to help her. She was grateful for that.

"No, I'll meet them at the funeral home."

"Ma'am." With a farewell dip of his head, the deputy turned away, leaving her standing there with a carrot in her hand.

Half an hour later and dressed in her doctor clothes, she arrived at Fuller's Funeral Home. And she wasn't the only visitor. Mr. McCormack's car sat parked beside another car she didn't recognize.

The blue Mountain High van wheeled into the parking lot just as she stepped out of her car.

"What are you doing here?" she asked as Guy popped out of the van and came around to where she waited. She couldn't help but feel relief at the sight of him. The woman in her wanted to lean against his tall, muscular frame, but the doctor in her kept a professional distance.

"Sheriff Potts called. It seems he's in touch with what's going on in his town."

The sheriff sent him? Horror at having lost the sheriff's support already almost sucked her into the black hole she had been circling since the deputy's news. "Does he think I'm responsible for Mr. Carter's death?"

Guy brushed her cheek with the back of his curled fingers, then let his hand fall quickly to his side. "He said he thought you might need some backup with McCormack and says he's sorry he didn't do something sooner about the man."

Caution. Okay. That was good. She nodded in acknowledgment. She'd been lucky in her encounters with

Mr. McCormack so far and Sheriff Potts knew it all the way from Kalispell.

"Did he ask you to be my bodyguard?"

"He just said he was worried and so I'm here to be whatever you need me to be."

She noticed the warmth in his eyes. She wanted to press herself to his chest and let him wrap his strong, protective arms around her, but if she let him solve her problems for her, she'd never be able to look herself in the face. "Thanks for coming."

When they entered the back door of the mortuary, several people fell silent. Mr. Fuller, the funeral director, and one of his sons greeted them. Mr. McCormack started toward Maude, but stepped back when he saw Guy. McCormack whispered something to a small, teary-eyed woman and then the woman approached Maude.

McCormack looked scary today. One chunk of his hair stuck out slightly from his slicked-back look.

"You have a lot of nerve coming here, Dr. DeVane." The woman's voice snapped her attention away from McCormack and to the woman's thin, worn face. She had a wild look of her own.

"I'm sorry, you must be related to Mr. Carter," Maude said, genuinely sympathetic for the woman.

"He's my brother." The woman glanced at McCormack who gave her sort of a *go ahead* nod. "He *was* my brother. How could you miss something so easy to see?"

Shelby Carter's sister would have stepped back had not McCormack stepped up and held her in place.

"I'm afraid I don't know what you're talking about." Shelby Carter's only obvious injury had been his hand.

"Of course you don't." This was McCormack, speaking

deliberately as if forcing his alcohol-soaked brain cells to work. "If you had examined him as he should have been examined, you could have saved his life. But you were too busy helping your friends, and you couldn't even have done that if it weren't for Dr. Daley here."

Guy moved up behind Maude and she could feel the anger radiating from him, but he said nothing.

Carter's sister stood beside McCormack bobbing her head up and down, until he finished speaking. Then she leveled an angry glare at Maude. "He's dead now and we can thank you for that."

"I tried to get you to admit you weren't a good enough…doctor." McCormack's words slurred a bit as he spoke.

"This isn't the time or place for this." Maude had to try.

"No, Maudie. It is the time and the place. You should leave the valley to someone who won't kill anybody else."

Maude let McCormack's words slide off her. She drew strength from Guy's presence and his willingness to let her handle things no matter how they came down.

Carter's sister leaned into McCormack who had pulled her closer as she began to cry. The funeral director's son stepped forward then to escort the pair of them to, "…someplace more comfortable."

"Dr. DeVane?"

Maude turned toward the funeral director. "Yes, Mr. Fuller."

"I thought you should see this."

He led them to the next room where Shelby Carter lay stretched out, covered by a green sheet except for his head. Mr. Fuller lifted the sheet far enough for Maude and Guy to see the marks on the man's chest, the kind of marks made when a body slams into a steering wheel during impact, such as the one with the Sandersons' van.

Maude took a ragged breath and Guy put a hand on her shoulder. The sight of the bruising on Mr. Carter's body did more to undermine Maude's calm than anything Mr. McCormack could have ever said.

"Thank you, Mr. Fuller."

She made herself march calmly from the building to her car. When she got there, she turned to Guy. "I could not have missed something like that."

"Not even if you were blind, Maude." He leaned over and opened the door of her car.

"But somehow I did." She looked up to see what she could find in his face.

He leaned in and kissed her. "I'll follow you home."

"I'm fine. I don't need to be coddled." Anger niggled, but it wasn't Guy's fault.

"I do."

He looked so serious, she smiled and stroked his cheek. A sudden rush of warmth spread through her at the thought of mussed white bedding and taut muscles. "Maybe you should follow me home. My parents are still in Great Falls with Sally's children until sometime tomorrow."

A FEW HOURS LATER they sat at the kitchen table sipping warm tea. The warm glow of lovemaking with Guy had filled her, but soon the contentment ebbed.

"Did I give everything I had to the Sandersons and not leave enough for the person who caused the accident in the first place?"

"He refused to let you examine him."

"Should I have tried harder?"

"Do you think you should have?"

"No. Abby and I both tried to convince him, but…" Uneasiness filtered in, a dreadful realization filled her head. "Even if I did everything right. Even if I never made a mistake in my life, what if I never find a way to get this valley of people to accept me?"

He held her hand and offered no platitudes, because that's what they'd be.

"They're not bad people, really. They just need to understand me and…have a man for a doctor." A hard knot formed in her stomach when she thought about Sammy McCormack. The child almost died because his parents had no faith in her, and she thought about all the others who felt the need to drive to Kalispell for medical care rather than rely on her. And kids like Sammy didn't get to choose their fate at all.

"I can't force them to accept me. What if 'do no harm' means I should leave this valley to find someone they can trust?"

"What would you do if you left?"

"I don't know. Go back to Chicago, to the clinic I worked at there." She could throw herself at Guy and be a failure who needed to be shored up for the rest of her life. Not exactly the way to make a man like Guy fall in love with her. "Doctors Without Borders suddenly seems like a good idea."

"I've heard the work can suck you dry, but the people are grateful."

He sounded far away when he spoke. Did he miss practicing medicine? "What about you?"

"I would like to tell you I could see the future, yours or mine, but…" He gently stroked her fingers. "Right now, I have an image to maintain in the eyes of a twelve-year-old, so I have to get to the ranch."

She saw him to the door and went upstairs and crawled under the covers.

*Do no harm* marched relentlessly through her head until she knew leaving the valley was her only alternative. She brought the covers up around her ears and since she was leaving there was no need to make nice. She could sleep all weekend, so no one—

*Oh God.* She tossed off the covers and sat up.

Sunday was the annual All Valley Picnic.

The ice-cream social where people filtered in and out quickly had been bad enough, but how could she face an entire afternoon of fun and games with the whole town's population?

How could she not?

She settled back and yanked the covers over her chilly body. What better place to say goodbye and thank you to everyone. No muss, no fuss, a group *adios* and she could be on her way to whatever the future held.

And leave the man she loved, in the valley she loved.

SATURDAY DAWNED rainy gray.

Later, in town, Guy turned his collar up against the cold rain and made his way from the hardware store to the drugstore where Lexie was no doubt filling bags hand over little fist. The day might be gray but what Guy planned to tell Lexie later would bring sunshine into her life. St. Margaret's was as good as any place out there to work. Especially if it gave Maude the chance she needed here in St. Adelbert.

Lexie smiled at him when he entered the store and held up four bags. "I got everything."

"Do they have anything left to sell the next customer?"

She rolled her eyes at him. "Men just don't get it."

"I suspect you're right about that. Let's eat." He held the door open for her.

"Alice's?" she threw over her shoulder.

"I thought we'd go back to the ranch and eat lunch."

She stopped and glared at him and then fled for the diner.

The last time he fed her lunch when Bessie was off, he was informed cereal for lunch was *mean*.

After lunch, he'd take her back to the ranch and tell her they were leaving. He'd have told her before they came to town, but he was never sure how she'd react to anything and wasn't sure she'd keep quiet about it. He needed to tell Maude, make sure she knew he wasn't deserting her.

As he and Lexie sat in the diner, more than one person felt obliged to stop by the table to tell him Shel Carter had died. It didn't seem to bother them a child was present, but only the first one got the chance to speak his piece. It was good to know his authoritative doctor stare still worked. He was going to need it in Chicago, along with his lab coat, mobile phone and hospital pager. Although, even with all those things, he knew he could never return to his old life.

Yes, some of the people of St. Adelbert were old-fashioned by his standards, but he was going to miss this valley and its doctor as well.

He wanted to stop and see Maude, find out how she was doing. He'd left her a message at her home this morning, but she hadn't returned his call. Now he didn't want to drag Lexie into the fray any deeper than she already was, so he took the girl back to the ranch.

By the time they got home, Lexie was grumpy and he didn't feel much better himself.

"But Maude couldn't have done anything wrong," Lexie insisted as they built a fire in the fireplace in the living room to rid the house of the rainy chill.

"She didn't." Guy let Lexie light the fire.

"Then you go tell them."

"I'm afraid, Lexie, that I'm part of the problem for Dr. DeVane here in the valley."

"But you're her friend, aren't you?"

"I am, and I have something important to tell you."

"You're going to let me order that PC game online?" She smiled brightly at him as if she knew he was going to tell her something dire.

"It's good news."

"Oh." She blew out a breath and fell back on her elbows. "Lay it on me. Good news I can take."

"I'm going to accept a job in Chicago."

"You're going to leave me here on the ranch by myself?"

"No. No. No," he said quickly, responding to the look of horror on her face. "We're moving back to Chicago, you and me."

She jumped to her feet. "No."

"What?" He'd have to be deaf and blind to be any worse at reading this child.

"No, I don't want to go. The ranch is mine and it's all I have. I don't want to go."

"Two days ago, you wanted to have Jake tie Timber up at the Old Water Tower, and give the ranch to your grandparents."

"Becca is coming back from her grandparents' in California next week."

"Becca?" Guy wondered if he was supposed to know who Becca was.

Lexie put her hands on her hips. "The only really, really good friend I have in the world lives here. I went to school out here for a while, remember." Her hands moved up to grab handfuls of curls as if she might need to pull them out in frustration because he was so stupid. "I'd never meet someone like her in Chicago." She plopped down on the floor beside him and held her hands out to the growing fire.

"The thing is." Guy spoke as gently as he could. "If I leave, the people here will learn to appreciate Maude. Right now, they want me to be the doctor. They think I'd be better than Maude, but they're wrong. She's as good as I am and deserves a chance here without competition from a—a friend."

"Well, just don't be a doctor here." She looked up at him.

"I tried that. It didn't work very well."

She sat quietly, chin in her hands, elbows on her knees, staring into the fire.

"I'll go," she said eventually.

"What?"

The look she shot at him held both innocence and pleading. "Because if I have a family, I suppose I can always make friends."

"Did anyone ever tell you, you're a great kid, Lexie?"

"My dad did."

"Of course, he did." He mentally hugged her. "We can fly your friend back to visit us on holidays. I'll bring you here to see her once in a while."

She scowled up at him. "Yeah, that'll happen."

"All right, I'll get Kelly to bring you and Adam out here. Bessie would help take care of Adam, and his mother will get a break, and you and your friend can put on all the makeup Kelly will let you, as long as you scrub it all off before you come back home."

But that didn't seem to make her happy, either, and then to his horror, she put her face in her hands and began to cry.

"Lexie." He scooted across the carpet to sit close to her.

"Uncle Guy." She looked up at him with tears in her big blue eyes.

It was a good thing she hadn't figured out he'd give her anything she wanted when she looked at him like that. "Yes, Lexie."

She scrubbed at the tears with both fists and sniffed. "Can I be your daughter?"

He dropped his hand to the floor behind her, but didn't touch her. "Yes, Lexie. I'd be honored if you would be my daughter."

Hand on her chin, she studied the fire for a while.

"Dad? Pops? Daddy? My old man?" She made a face after each one she tried and then sighed exaggeratedly. "Can I still call you 'Uncle Guy' even if I'm your daughter?"

"That would be good, and definitely 'my old man' is out."

She pushed to her knees and held her hand up for a high five. He obliged.

"Thanks, Uncle Guy, and there's one more thing."

"I'm not buying you a red sports car."

She gave him a teary smile. "I won't be needing one of those until I'm sixteen."

"Okay, then what."

"Before we go, you need to see Maude. You need to tell

her—those people at the restaurant. What's wrong with them? Maude didn't kill anybody. Even I know that."

"You're right, Maude didn't hurt anyone. Even I couldn't outshine her the night of the accident."

"Not even you?" She gave him an exaggerated look of incredulity.

"Smart aleck."

"Well, you need to tell her we think she's a great doctor."

"I'll go see her."

"Good, and I'd like one now."

"You'd like one what?" Now what had he missed?

"A hug."

He laughed and folded her into his arms. "I love you, Lexie Daley." He smoothed the mop of red curls pressed against his chin. "Hey, we won't even have to change your name, unless you'd like to be Delilah Daley or Cameron Daley or Brittney Daley or…"

She hugged him fiercely. "Lexie Daley is good. But go see Maude now. I'm worried about her. Tell her I'll miss her and she'll have to visit me."

"I'll do that."

"Now go. Go." She pushed him until he stood.

As Guy shrugged into his jacket, he had to admit he was worried about Maude, and he had to admit, he might be more worried about himself. If he left the valley or he stayed, he was going to lose the woman he loved.

Maude DeVane. A month ago he would have thought she was the last person on earth he could ever have feelings for and now he had to walk away or watch her slowly break under the pressure of never being able to believe in herself.

THE SHARP RINGING of her phone brought Maude out of a restless nap. Her parents' home phone number appeared in the caller ID window. "Hello, Mom."

"Hello, dear."

Maude blinked several times to try to wake up. "When are you coming back here? I thought you wanted to go to the picnic."

"We do, and we are, but I'd like to talk to you about Amanda."

A deep-seated trepidation made its way to the surface. "What's wrong? Has something happened to her?"

"I went to see her today. I just wanted to see her."

"Why?" Her mother never visited Amanda unless she had to.

"I wanted to tell her I love her, and I want to tell you something."

"I'm listening, Mom?" The trepidation heightened.

"I got up that night—" Her mother paused.

"The night of the storm?" *I don't want you to talk about that ever again.* Her mother's words echoed inside her head.

"Yes. I got up and if I'd have just checked on my girls. If I had just gone in to give you each a kiss that night. I did that, you know. Kissed you when you were asleep sometimes."

"I know, Mom. We weren't always asleep… Mom?"

"Yes, dear?"

"I took your ring."

"I know, dear."

"Amanda thought she should have stopped me from taking it. I took your most precious possession and I lost it in the snow. I'm sorry."

"But, Maude—"

"If I had just told you. If I had known she went out—"

"Maude!"

"What, Mother?"

"The ring was never my most precious possession. Maude, the most precious things in my life are and always were my daughters."

"Thanks, Mom. Hearing you say that means more than you'll ever know. I love you. I'll see you tomorrow at the picnic."

"Yes, dear, your father and I will be there and we love you, too."

Maude put the phone back on the hook. Her mother knew she had taken the ring. All these years, her mother knew…and felt the guilt of responsibility for what had happened to Amanda. Maybe, sometimes accidents did just happen. As Maude wandered upstairs for a shower, a sense of calm about her sister began to replace the unrelenting pain.

The doorbell rang an hour later. She had showered and dressed, but her hair hung in damp locks and there was no one in town she wanted to see.

But she would see someone from the ranch, she thought as she opened the door and let Guy inside.

"Hi." She suddenly felt shy. What could she really say to him? That she had given up?

"Lexie wanted me to come and see if you were all right. *I* wanted to come and see."

"Come in. I was just about to fix a snack. Have a seat."

He nodded and sat at the kitchen table.

"I have to leave the valley," Maude said as she came and sat down with a plate of cheese and fruit for them.

"No. I have to go. The other night showed me, Maude.

I have to practice medicine, and you have to stay. If the people here give you a chance, they'll learn to trust you."

"They trusted you from the start."

"It was a knee-jerk response to my being a male. They didn't know me at all."

"They knew me too well."

"Can you come to Chicago with Lexie and me?"

She studied him thoughtfully. "I can't. I thought I knew what I wanted, I was so sure."

"You still want the same thing."

"But I can't have it."

"I wasn't talking about practicing in the valley, but it would probably be the best place for you."

"Because if I could get these people to trust me, I'd trust myself?"

He nodded.

"I could find that somewhere else."

"You might, but you'd always wonder—"

"If my success at some big clinic in Chicago was just because I was one of the doctors people had to come to because their insurance company said so."

He raised his eyebrows. "Would that be enough for you?"

Would working at a clinic in Chicago be enough for her if she had Guy at her side at night?

Or rather, would it be enough for Guy to have an empty shell at his side at night? She knew the answer. She would leave St. Adelbert and find a clinic somewhere, but not in Chicago. When the day came that she had her head screwed on straight, maybe she could look him up.

He covered her hand with his and studied her with dark eyes probing. "I love you, you know."

"I love you." But she couldn't offer him the remains of

a woman. He needed someone strong, someone complete. Someone he could come home to after a grueling day and find strength and love, not neediness and doubt.

"And it's not enough, is it?"

She shook her head. "It might be for a while, but I need to be whole. I just realized, I haven't been whole since I was a kid. And you deserve better."

## CHAPTER TWELVE

BY ONE O'CLOCK Sunday afternoon, Maude had stood in front of her closet for half an hour trying to decide which would be her best goodbye outfit to wear to the picnic.

Tears streamed down her face. *Sorry, Sally.* She did still cry. Leaving the valley would be hard. Letting go of the man she loved with all her heart made the loss all the more painful.

The wound on her heart tore open a bit more as she felt the touch of Guy's lips on hers, his hands on her body, but mostly the look of understanding in his eyes when she spoke of Amanda and spoke of how she needed to trust herself.

She swiped at the tears still on her cheeks, tore off the blue oxford and tossed it on the bed. She knew it was stupid, bordering on ridiculous, to be analyzing what outfit she should wear to be run out of town, but it had to be done.

Three outfits, tried on and discarded, lay on her bed. She finally settled for old jeans with a hand-tooled belt, a light pink blouse, a white cardigan and her favorite old boots. She was going to look like one of them. If they were going to tell her goodbye, they were going to have to look one of their own in the eye, not a big-city doctor all spiffed up in city duds.

When the double chime of her front doorbell rang, she almost jumped out of her jeans. No one came to her front door. Oddly, she didn't care who it was. She stopped in the bathroom and dabbed her eyes with a cold cloth. Before she got down the stairs the doorbell chimed again.

Through the eyelet lace curtain on her front door she could see red hair. Mr. McCormack. *Icky.* The word had popped into her head unbidden. She laughed. He was icky. She thanked Lexie for the most appropriate word, and then she buried her smile and opened the door. "Good morning, Mr. McCormack."

He stood on the wide expanse of the front porch backed up by his minions: the other council member from last week's ice-cream social, Mr. Carter's sister and a few other people Maude knew from office visits and from the diner or grocery store.

"Dr. DeVane." McCormack jutted his chin out as he spoke. His hair was back in place this afternoon and he was dressed casually, picnic style, and he was very twitchy, probably in need of a drink. "We came by as a courtesy to you."

"A courtesy?" Maude gave him a pleasant smile, which seemed to increase his agitation, and then she gave the same smile to each person standing on her porch. Each quickly found someplace else to look.

"We've come to tell you it would be best if you didn't come to the picnic today." He reached up and picked at a chip of loose paint on the door frame.

She wanted to slap his hand and say, that's mine; don't touch it.

"Shel Carter was a friend to many of us," he continued, "and we suggest you stay away today so everyone can remember Shel the way he ought to be remembered."

She looked at Shelby Carter's sister. "I'm truly sorry for your loss. If there is anything I can do for you, please let me know."

"Now, see. That's the kind of thing we want to prevent this afternoon. We don't want your sympathy, and your offer for assistance is way too late."

"Mr. McCormack." She stepped out onto the porch so she stood in the middle of the crowd. "Will I ever make a mistake while I am practicing medicine? Yes. I will. I won't do it often and I will learn from each one of them. Every time I learn from a mistake, I will be a better, smarter doctor. I'm sorry, Mrs. Diaz, but your brother's death was not my mistake."

McCormack's face turned deep red. "You will be so sorry if you come this afternoon."

"Mr. McCormack, I'll be seeing you soon." She stepped back inside her house and closed the door firmly.

On her way back to her room, she found herself standing in front of the hallway mirror, staring…at her image. There were times when she treated herself no better than McCormack did. How could she do that? She lowered her eyes. She deserved better, especially from herself.

Slowly she raised her eyes to look herself in face. "I'm sorry, Maude. I'm going to change that, I promise." A rush of exhilarating emotion flooded into her as she realized she meant it. She was leaving for better things and she felt good about her prospects.

She felt so good, she went into her room and put on her expensive, big-city boots with stacked heels and two rows of buttons all the way up the front and a skirt to show them off.

An hour later, head held high, boots clicking in time to

her steps, she headed for the town square. The picnic would be in full swing. Tomorrow she might be crying into her pillow, but not today.

The lightness stayed with her until she got to the square and counted how many people were there. So many to say goodbye to, so many she would actually miss. A sadness settled into her heart, but not more than she could handle. She strode to the heart of the square.

Mr. Hawes, the man whose wife had died after suffering from Alzheimer's, greeted her with a big smile. "Dr. DeVane, it's good to see you."

"How are things going, Mr. Hawes?"

A woman stepped up beside him. "This is my wife's sister, Evelyn. We spent so much time together the last few years, well…we thought we should stay friends. It was you, Dr. DeVane, who made me realize I should follow my heart."

"I'm happy for both of you." Maude watched as the two of them walked away in animated conversation.

"Dr. 'Vane. Dr. 'Vane." She turned to see Charlie Thompson waving to her and running in her direction. His parents and his aunt Sarah followed him as he ran up to her. "We got a puppy. We got a puppy."

His father laughed and swept the little boy up into his arms. Maude could see how well the stitches in his head were healing. Guy had done a great job. Mrs. Thompson stood beside her husband and son and almost glowed with happiness.

"We thought Arabella could use a playmate," Mrs. Thompson said, and grinned at Maude. "Since Charlie's going to have one when the new baby is born. We'll be in to see you soon about that."

"Congratulations to all of you."

The happy family headed off. Maude felt a bit wistful that the next little Thompson would be birthed by whoever followed her as the valley's doctor.

This was harder than she'd thought it would be. Maybe if her parents were here, but those two were late as usual. And she couldn't even let herself think of Guy.

Across the square, Cole Dawson, one of the ranchers who'd searched for Lexie, and his fashion-model wife were being queried by the gossip sisters. She was sure Cole wished his horse would come and carry him off into the sunset, but his wife preened under the attention.

Baylor Doyle, the shameless flirt who had helped search for Lexie, was carrying on a spirited discussion with Abby over a game of horseshoes. Maude smiled. What a match those two would make.

"Think you're so smug, don't you?"

Without turning, she knew Mr. McCormack stood behind her. Even if he hadn't spoken, she could have smelled the booze.

"Dr. DeVane doesn't need your interference, Mr. McCormack."

The sound of the gravelly second voice made her spin in alarm. Curly Martin stood brandishing his pink cast at the drunken man.

Then she almost staggered back when she saw the big shadow behind Curly today was not the grandson, but Guy Daley.

Mr. McCormack tried to muster his courage, but instead, spun and strode unsteadily away.

"Sorry about him and his crew." Curly jerked a thumb at McCormack and the group of the town's people who gathered around him.

Maude folded her arms over her chest. "Curly Martin, you could have gotten yourself hurt, or worse."

He drew his brows together. "What do you care? Rumor says you're leaving."

"I just washed my lab coat and here I might have felt obliged to take you to the clinic and try to save you."

He smiled at her, but it quickly faded. "It's true then?"

"It's best if I leave. The people here need someone they can trust."

"I trust you."

When his quiet words made the tears prickle in her eyes, she forced out a rough, "Thank you."

Curly left to join Jimmy, and Guy stepped up and smiled at her. That lock of dark hair flopped down on his mountain-tanned forehead and she had to repress a shiver of elation. She wanted to banish the crowd and leave only Guy and her in the world. "I keep thinking each time I see you will be my last," she said.

"So you haven't changed your mind. There are people here who think the sun rises and sets with you, Dr. DeVane."

"A few, but not enough." She nodded at the growing knot of people around Mr. McCormack.

"He's the loud squeaky wheel. People might come around."

She shook her head. "The cost is too high."

His dark eyes studied her. She loved this man, but her resolve to walk away only strengthened.

"Dr. DeVane." The sound of her name came over the public address system. Maude looked up at the raised platform to see the mayor motioning for her to come up. Beside him stood a stranger, a man dressed in a suit, looking totally out of place at a picnic, but he was grinning eagerly.

*You'll be sorry*. McCormack's words echoed inside her head. Oh right, this fish-out-of-water-looking man must be her replacement.

The mayor smiled down at her. He had never had an unkind word to say to her. He was one of the people she had thought might give her a chance. Now he wanted to haul her up on stage and introduce her to the man who would live her dream. Well, at least she'd show them she was a good loser.

"Come on up, Dr. DeVane." He pointed to the side of the stage where the steps were.

Once she was on the platform, the mayor motioned her over. "This is Dr. Kilmer. I thought the two of you should meet."

McCormack and his group, standing several yards to the side, turned as one to face her.

The sooner this was over, the better. She straightened her spine and stuck out her hand. "Welcome, Dr. Kilmer." Once the handshake was over, she asked for the microphone. "I wanted to thank everyone who was so kind to me. You are a great bunch of people, and Dr. Kilmer will be happy here, I'm sure. I hope I get a chance to come back someday."

Maude stopped. A murmur started at the back of the square and like the Red Sea, the crowd parted. To her delight, a healthy-looking and uniformed Sheriff Potts strode toward the stage with his smiling wife and children in his wake. Many hands clapped him on the back as he passed. Maybe she would never have achieved the kind of status the sheriff had in the community, but "Old Doc DeVane" might have been good.

Sheriff Potts stepped up onto the stage without the benefit of the steps, and faced the crowd, who cheered the returning sheriff as they might have a conquering hero.

"Thank you." He made a nervous bow as the cheering increased. "Thank you. Now cut it out." Laughter peppered the clapping and soon the crowd was quietly attentive. "I have something I need to tell everyone."

He turned toward Maude and covered the microphone, "Thought I'd do this in public. The gossip network in this valley has done enough damage since I left."

Maude had no idea what he was going to "do," but Sheriff Potts had a way of arousing confidence. She gazed out over the crowd without pausing on any of the faces. If she looked at Guy, she might have to jump off the stage and into his arms.

Maybe it would have been better if she had left without seeing him again. She never thought of herself as a sloppy sentimental person, but with him, she could see herself getting that way, often.

The sheriff cleared his throat. "I wanted all of you to hear this from the horse's mouth."

A few chuckles rose from the crowd along with some rib poking.

"There was nothing wrong with Shelby Carter when he left Dr. DeVane's care except the cut on his hand." Murmuring from the crowd. "Shel was involved in another car accident after they let him out of jail. Now you know I can't confirm or deny any of the details of the accident until the investigation is complete, so you folks go ahead and make up anything you want." He searched the crowd almost as if he were making eye contact with each one of them. "I am one hundred percent sure Dr. DeVane was not responsible for Shel Carter's death."

With that, he stepped away from the microphone and gestured for Maude to finish.

Maude knew this should feel like a white knight had

charged in to her rescue, but the news changed nothing. She still had to do what was best for the valley. If Shelby Carter had been the issue, things would be solved and she'd send Dr. Kilmer packing.

At least McCormack had disappeared from the square. She hoped someone, maybe Dr. Kilmer, could help the man before he hurt himself or his wife and children.

"Thank you, Sheriff Potts. I am truly sorry for Shelby Carter's passing and I wish there had been a better outcome for him." She bowed her head for a moment, partly for Mr. Carter and partly because she was about to abandon what had at first been Amanda's dream. *Sorry, Amanda.* And then it had been her own. "I'd like to say goodbye to the good people of the St. Adelbert valley. And I'd like to help the mayor welcome—"

"Bawk." At the loud imitation of a chicken cluck many people laughed.

"—to welcome—"

This time there were a few more clucks and some squawks.

She just wanted to get this done, so she took a breath and opened her mouth to speak and the square erupted in chicken sounds, someone even crowed like a rooster. She could see the leader emerge from the crowd.

Curly. He could defend her honor, but he wanted her gone like so many did. Sadness overcame. Cackles and squawks; it was better, she supposed, than boos and hisses.

When he got close to the stage, she peered down. "Curly, of all the people here, I would have thought you might, as least, wish me well."

His shocking response was to grin at her. "You're a big yellow chicken."

"I thought you—"

He grinned wider.

"What are you smiling about?"

She looked out at the crowd. Every damn one of them was grinning at her, including Lexie and Guy, and beside them, Jake and Bessie and Bessie's daughter. When she turned, even the sheriff was smiling.

The mayor stepped forward. "I think what Mr. Martin is so indelicately trying to say is, we didn't all want you gone, Dr. DeVane, but if you had wanted out of your commitment, we were willing to let you go."

"Wanted out?"

"I apologize for the confusion, on behalf of the whole council. Mr. McCormack was apparently untruthful with us and also with you. It seems, when he told you the lies, he allowed you to believe he spoke for all of us. I assure you he did not."

"I, um, I— What about Dr. Kilmer?" Her stammering words echoed through the sound system. She clamped her mouth shut before she said anything too ridiculous.

Standing at the foot of the stage next to Guy and Lexie were her parents, with Sally between them. Maude's mother leaned over and said something to Guy, who nodded.

"Dr. DeVane, we knew you'd be too busy…" She heard the mayor speaking and gave him her full attention. "…to find someone to back you up. Even Doc Avery had his brother…in a pinch. So we finally found someone willing to help out from time to time."

"I don't know what to say." She looked from the mayor to Dr. Kilmer.

"You can say you'll stay."

Maude couldn't breathe. Things were, once again, standing on their head. Leave. Stay. Leave. Stay. In a blur of unreality she felt her head bobbing up and down and then "yes" slipped out between her lips. Even as she said the word, she knew it would mean saying goodbye to Guy and Lexie forever when they went back to Chicago.

The mayor nodded to the crowd. "And if it's all right with you, Dr. Kilmer here would love to come out from New York and be your replacement when you need a vacation." Dr. Kilmer grinned. This seemed much to his liking.

"Or a honeymoon." someone from the front of the crowd called.

Maude spotted Sally winking and grinning up at her. Maude blushed and glanced down at Guy who grinned.

"Dr. Daley."

Guy seemed shocked to be singled out by a shout from the crowd, but he stepped forward and turned to face the group.

"What exactly are your intentions for our Doc?" a young man hollered.

Then another voice did the same. "Yeah, what are your intentions for our Doc?"

*They called me Doc!* was the first thing to register. But the revelry going on in her head was flat-out banished by the realization they were demanding of Guy to know if he was going to marry her.

"We want to know *now,* Dr. Daley." Sally chortled. Several others chimed in with "Yes, tell us," and "We wanna know," and such.

Guy turned to Lexie. The two of them conferred for a moment, probably trying figure out how to escape before the crowd got too testy. Then he reached out to Lexie and, miracle of miracles, she grabbed his hand.

Then, the two of them strode off toward the street.

They were leaving, walking right out of her life. Of course, they were leaving. In a moment they would be running as fast as they could back to civilization.

In a panic, Maude knew she was going to be left standing on the stage, rejected in front of God and valley.

The pair suddenly veered from their path and up the steps onto the stage, where they stopped directly in front of her. In unison, they each dropped to one knee.

She gaped at them while the crowd hooted and cheered.

"Maude," Lexie started and then tugged on her uncle Guy's arm.

The crowd went absolutely silent.

"Maude." His deep voice swept over her as he said her name, and she had to stiffen her knees to keep from collapsing where she stood. "Lexie and I would like to know if you will marry us and share your valley with us."

Maude looked out at the expanse of the upturned faces and then between Guy and Lexie. Lexie beamed. Maude had never seen her happier, and Guy curled his lips into a warm smile.

In a loud stage whisper he said, "Apparently we're an item."

She feigned a shocked expression.

He whispered again, "If you stand behind the canned peas display long enough, you can find out anything. So, will you marry me?"

With choking emotion rising in her throat, she squeaked out, "Yes, I'll marry you." And then, "Will you share my practice with me, Dr. Daley?"

"I will, Dr. DeVane."

Guy took her left hand and gently opened her clenched fist. When he slid her grandmother's ruby ring on her finger, she couldn't hold back a sob.

Cheers and hoots peppered the wild clapping and several people whistled when he held up her hand for them to see. Someone set off a firecracker. Although none of the pandemonium around her compared to the celebration going on inside her heart.

Lexie and Guy swept her into a family embrace.

"You're hugging now?" she asked Lexie.

Lexie's response was to hug tighter.

A "Kiss the Doc" chant soon swept through the crowd like the clinking of knife blades on glasses at a wedding reception.

Maude saw Curly and Jimmy chanting. And her mother and her father chanting, and the rascal Sally, whom she suspected was responsible for inciting the crowd, chanting and laughing.

Guy pulled Maude to him and kissed her soundly and the valley disappeared.

When she opened her eyes again she remembered they were surrounded.

She hugged Lexie again.

"I'm going to call him Uncle Guy, but can I call you Mom?"

Maude looked up at Guy who grinned and lifted one shoulder. She touched the bouncy red curls. "I'd be so happy if you did, Lexie."

Then Maude hugged her parents. Sally came next. "Thank you, Maude. I will pay you back for saving my family for the rest of my life."

"I'm so glad I'll be here to collect."

Jake stepped up and she saw in his face the most emotion she'd ever seen in him. She even imagined a small tear stood in the corner of one eye. "Welcome, home, Dr. DeVane." She hugged him hard.

Bessie was crying and even her daughter smiled.

When she hugged Curly he said, "Nice boots, Doc." And Jimmy smelled faintly of firecrackers.

When she looked up at the next hugger, Lexie was back in line. "I've got some catching up to do."

When Lexie moved away, Guy moved back in, and as he took her in his arms the sky opened up and rain poured down on them. Shrieks and shouts rose around them followed by the thudding of running feet.

"Come on, Lexie," Maude heard Sally call to the girl.

Guy held Maude and kissed her again.

She pushed back in the tight circle of his arms. "Don't you think we should get in out of the rain?"

"I like rain. I have for many years," he said as he gazed into her eyes. "It was raining the first time I kissed you in Chicago and the first time I kissed you in St. Adelbert."

She smiled her happiness at him.

He smiled back. "And, for the rest of my life, every time it rains, Maude, I'm going to kiss you. I love you, Doc."

"Let it rain then. Let it pour because I love you, too, Doc."

"This must be what you meant when you said I deserved better."

She grinned and nodded and he lowered his mouth to hers.

* * * * *

*In honor of our 60th anniversary,*
*Harlequin® American Romance® is celebrating*
*by featuring an all-American male each month,*
*all year long with*
**MEN MADE IN AMERICA!**
*This June, we'll be featuring American men*
*living in the West.*

*Here's a sneak preview of*
*THE CHIEF RANGER by Rebecca Winters.*

*Chief Ranger Vance Rossiter has to confront the sister of*
*a man who died while under Vance's watch...and also*
*confront his attraction to her.*

"Chief Ranger Rossiter?" The sight of the woman who'd stepped inside Vance's office brought him to his feet. "I'm Rachel Darrow. Your secretary said I should come right in."

"Please," he said, walking around his desk to shake her hand. At a glance he estimated she was in her midtwenties. Her feminine curves did wonders for the pale blue T-shirt and jeans she was wearing. "Ranger Jarvis informed me there's a young boy with you."

The unfriendly expression in her beautiful green eyes caught him off guard. "Yes," was her clipped reply. "When we arrived in Yosemite the ranger told me I couldn't go anywhere in the park until I talked to you first."

"That's right."

"Knowing you wanted this meeting to be private, he offered to show my nephew around Headquarters."

So this woman was the victim's sister… "What's his name?"

"Nicky."

The boy who haunted Vance's dreams now had a name. "How old is he?"

"He turned six three weeks ago. Were you the man in charge when my brother and sister-in-law were killed?"

"Yes. To tell you I'm sorry for what happened couldn't begin to convey my feelings."

The woman's gaze didn't flicker. "I won't even try to describe mine. Just tell me one thing. Was their accident preventable?"

"Yes," he answered without hesitation.

"In other words, the people working under you fell asleep on your watch and two lives were snuffed out as a result."

Hearing it put like that, he had to set the record straight. "My staff had nothing to do with it. I, myself, could have prevented the loss of life."

Ms. Darrow's expression hardened. "So you admit culpability."

"Yes. I take full blame."

A look of pain crossed over her features. "You can just stand there and admit it?" Her cry echoed that of his own tortured soul.

"Yes." He sucked in his breath.

"I work for a cruise line. Aboard ship, it's the captain's responsibility to maintain rigid safety regulations. If a disaster like that had happened while he was in charge he would have been relieved of his command and never given another ship again."

Rachel Darrow couldn't know she was preaching to the converted. "If you've come to the park with the intention of bringing a lawsuit against me for negligence, maybe you should." It would only be what he deserved.

"Maybe I will."

In the next instant, she wheeled around and hurried out of his office. Vance could have gone after her, but it would cause a scene, something he was loath to do for a variety of reasons. In the first place, he needed to cool down before he approached her again.

The discovery of the Darrows' frozen bodies had affected every ranger in the park. A little boy had been orphaned—a boy whose aunt was all he had left.

* * * * *

*Will Rachel allow Vance to explain—and will*
*she let him into her heart?*
*Find out in*
**THE CHIEF RANGER**
*Available June 2009 from*
*Harlequin® American Romance®.*

We'll be spotlighting a different series every month
throughout 2009 to celebrate our 60th anniversary.

## Look for Harlequin®
## American Romance® in June!

Join us for a year-long celebration of the rugged
American male! From cops to cowboys—
Men Made in America has the hero
you've been dreaming about!

Look for

# The Chief Ranger

by Rebecca Winters, on sale in June!

---

---

www.eHarlequin.com                    HARBPA09

# Escape Around the World

*Dream destinations, whirlwind weddings!*

# Honeymoon with the Boss

*by*

# JESSICA HART

Top tycoon Tom Maddison is used to calling the shots—until his convenient marriage falls through. But rather than waste his honeymoon, he'll take his boardroom to the beach and bring his oh-so-sensible secretary Imogen on a tropical business trip! But will Tom finally see the sexy woman that prudent Imogen truly is?

*Available in June wherever books are sold.*

# REQUEST YOUR FREE BOOKS!
## 2 FREE NOVELS PLUS 2 FREE GIFTS!

HARLEQUIN®

*Super Romance*®

## Exciting, emotional, unexpected!

**YES!** Please send me 2 FREE Harlequin® Superromance® novels and my 2 FREE gifts (gifts are worth about $10). After receiving them, if I don't wish to receive any more books, I can return the shipping statement marked "cancel." If I don't cancel, I will receive 6 brand-new novels every month and be billed just $4.69 per book in the U.S. or $5.24 per book in Canada. That's a savings of close to 15% off the cover price! It's quite a bargain! Shipping and handling is just 50¢ per book*. I understand that accepting the 2 free books and gifts places me under no obligation to buy anything. I can always return a shipment and cancel at any time. Even if I never buy another book from Harlequin, the two free books and gifts are mine to keep forever.

135 HDN EYLG   336 HDN EYLS

| | | |
|---|---|---|
| Name | (PLEASE PRINT) | |
| Address | | Apt. # |
| City | State/Prov. | Zip/Postal Code |

Signature (if under 18, a parent or guardian must sign)

### Mail to the **Harlequin Reader Service**:
**IN U.S.A.:** P.O. Box 1867, Buffalo, NY 14240-1867
**IN CANADA:** P.O. Box 609, Fort Erie, Ontario  L2A 5X3

Not valid to current subscribers of Harlequin Superromance books.

**Are you a current subscriber of Harlequin Superromance books
and want to receive the larger-print edition?
Call 1-800-873-8635 today!**

* Terms and prices subject to change without notice. Prices do not include applicable taxes. Sales tax applicable in N.Y. Canadian residents will be charged applicable provincial taxes and GST. Offer not valid in Quebec. This offer is limited to one order per household. All orders subject to approval. Credit or debit balances in a customer's account(s) may be offset by any other outstanding balance owed by or to the customer. Please allow 4 to 6 weeks for delivery. Offer available while quantities last.

**Your Privacy:** Harlequin is committed to protecting your privacy. Our Privacy Policy is available online at www.eHarlequin.com or upon request from the Reader Service. From time to time we make our lists of customers available to reputable third parties who may have a product or service of interest to you. If you would prefer we not share your name and address, please check here. ☐

HSR09R

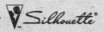

# SPECIAL EDITION

FROM *USA TODAY* BESTSELLING AUTHOR

# MARIE FERRARELLA

## THE ALASKANS

## LOVING THE RIGHT BROTHER

When tragedy struck, Irena Yovich headed
back to Alaska to console her ex-boyfriend's
family. While there she began seeing his brother,
Brody Hayes, in a very different light. Things
were about to really heat up. Had she fallen
for the wrong brother?

*Available in June
wherever books are sold.*

SSE65458

# HARLEQUIN *Super Romance*

## COMING NEXT MONTH

### Available June 9, 2009

**#1566 A SMALL-TOWN HOMECOMING • Terry McLaughlin**
*Built to Last*
The return of architect Tess Roussel to her hometown has put her on a collision course with John Jameson Quinn. The contractor has her reeling…his scandalous past overshadows everything. Tess wants to believe that the contractor is deserving of her professional admiration and her trust, but her love, too?

**#1567 A HOLIDAY ROMANCE • Carrie Alexander**
A summer holiday in the desert? What had Alice Potter been thinking? If it wasn't for resort manager Kyle Jarreau, her dream vacation would be a nightmare. But can they keep their fling a secret…? For Kyle's sake, they *have* to.

**#1568 FROM FRIEND TO FATHER • Tracy Wolff**
Reece Sandler never planned to raise his daughter with Sarah Martin. They were only friends when she agreed to be his surrogate. Now things have changed and they have to be parents—together. Fine. Easy. But only if Reece can control his attraction to Sarah.

**#1569 BEST FOR THE BABY • Ann Evans**
*9 Months Later*
Pregnant and alone, Alaina Tillman returns to Lake Harmony and Zack Davidson, her girlhood love. Yet as attracted as she is to him, life isn't just about the two of them anymore. She has to do what's best for her baby. Does that mean letting Zack in—or pushing him away?

**#1570 NO ORDINARY COWBOY• Mary Sullivan**
*Home on the Ranch*
A ranch is so not Amy Graves's scene. Still, she promised to help, so here she is. Funny thing is she starts to feel at home. And even funnier, she starts to fall for a cowboy— Hank Shelter. As she soon discovers, however, there's nothing ordinary about him.

**#1571 ALL THAT LOVE IS • Ginger Chambers**
*Everlasting Love*
Jillian Davis was prepared to walk away from her marriage. But when her husband, Brad, takes her on a shortcut, an accident nearly kills them. Now, with the SUV as their fragile shelter, Jillian's only hope lies with the man she was ready to leave behind forever.…

HSRCNMBPA0509